The Paradox Man

K. C. Banner

Dedication

To Grandma God Bless, Thank You for always encouraging my writing x

Prologue

What if you could go back in time and reverse every awful thing that had ever happened? If you could eliminate pain and suffering as you saw fit? Stop the bad things before they even happened, and give people more time with those they love? With the C.A.L.I.G.O device this is all possible, and the Ministry of Time oversees its proper, safe, and effective use. The Ministry must act outside the realms of public knowledge to protect what others may see as a weapon and use for selfish reasons. They are a secret guardian protecting and improving our history, carefully guiding humanity to its glorious future.

This is what successful applicants to the Ministry of Time are told on their first day of induction. For Michael Brown this was no different, and his faith in the Ministry had been unshakable from that day until today. After all what reason was there to doubt their altruism? They were everything one would expect of a government department charged with the protection of a miracle; they were secretive, public serving, and heavily overseen at several different levels of government. Yet, it seemed now that much of this had been a lie.

Michael glanced back up at the tv, where the only headline, on all channels, around the world, was the revelation of not only the invention of successful Time

Travel, but that those charged with the protection of this miracle had been using it for their personal gain. The politicians and Directors in command of the Ministry had had their dirty hands all over modern history; using their influence over the technological marvel of C.A.L.I.G.O to further their own interests. They had become wealthy men accumulating dominance and power over the modern world, so powerful in fact they were more akin to Gods than their fellow men; revered and envied by their colleagues as they eliminated free will to line their pockets.

The world was understandably in chaos after the exposé, as British allies demanded answers as to why they had not been informed that the British Government was in possession of such a revolutionary weapon. While their enemies made threats of war if nothing was done to bring the country and its government to justice.

Former and current politicians and businessmen linked to the corruption of the Ministry of Time, and its unethical use of the C.A.L.I.G.O device, were being called on to stand trial for their crimes. With each name that appeared on new reports, the pillars on which the country stood crumbled a little more. In the span of just a few short hours all trust the public had in their elected officials was destroyed and the country lay fractured and divided in the wake of their betrayal.

The world wanted answers to questions that hadn't even existed yesterday, as classified documents revealed that modern history had been moulded and guided in favour of those in trusted positions of power. Some other, more philosophical questions were being raised, several of which stretched back as far as ancient times, surrounding topics as great and grave as free will and autonomy.

Michael, like everyone else who worked for the Ministry, was currently sat in the canteen watching various screens with different examples of confidential documents, articles, and news reports. Needless to say, everyone implicated was playing it very close to their chest, as they refused to give themselves away as having participated in this egregious abuse of power. People around Michael spoke in hushed whispers, asking seemingly the most important question, that sat at the very centre of the issue. "Just who had revealed their existence to the world?" There were many theories circulating about who this enemy of the state was; or if they were even an enemy at all. At the very best they intended to destroy the Ministry and expose its alleged wrongdoings, at worst they hoped to throw Britain into war and destroy every aspect of government and trust.

Some bright spark had already pointed out that they could, of course, take the C.A.L.I.G.O device back to yesterday, and simply stop the information from being leaked in the first place. Which was fine in theory, but without knowing who the source of the leak was, where in the world they were, or for how long they had possessed this information, going back in time was rather useless. The next problem was that they had not been warned about the leak from the future, which typically indicated that this event was meant to happen. So, in the light of their exposure, for the first time in nearly forty years, the Ministry of Time was unsure of their future; and for the first time in nearly fifteen years, Michael Brown was definitely unsure of his.

June 22nd, 1972

Often when I think back to the triumphs of men and women detailed in the history books there is a certain level of heroism attributed to their advancements, they are heralded as beings before their time, God-like in their ability to launch humanity from one age to another in the span of a lifetime. These individuals achieve in one length of human existence, what could not be achieved by millions of their fellow men in centuries. However, for many of these heroes and visionaries they are not appreciated in the time they are born in. They do not experience the wealth of adoration and debts of gratitude that are owed to them, usually due to an untimely death on their part. Perhaps it is God's cruel reminder that although these few may be bestowed with gifts and knowledge beyond those of their kin, and they may for a moment touch the pure starlight that is the very universe, they are not truly gods and remain the mere mortals they fear themselves to be.

*I, myself, have always admired these great men and women of old whose mighty deeds and inventions fill the pages of dusty books on forgotten shelves; but I had my sights set on defying that convention of missing out, especially on what is perhaps the best part of public service. After all what is the point of furthering and enhancing the lives of your fellow men, if you do not receive the worship and recognition, you have rightfully earned. I had no designs on being a god-like man, that was how we were already born, in **his** image. No, I wanted to be a man-like God. I wanted to challenge the great overseer himself. I wanted a religion devoted to me. I wanted my life documented and recorded as a holy text.*

These days I see the foolishness of such a desire, it is selfish and prideful, and only now do I see the pitfalls; such is the nature of wisdom. Wisdom has perhaps become the cruellest gift I have gained in my Godhood, because only now can I see all the plethora of mistakes I have made, a side-effect of my weak humanity. I made the mistake as a young man, of assuming wisdom and intelligence were the same thing. I was after all highly intelligent and considered all round a very bright young man, one who had the potential to move the world lightyears ahead in its advancement. So, what was wisdom except another word for intellect? And who were these nobodies who had achieved nothing in their unremarkable lives to tell me otherwise?

My plan, to accomplish my all too human desires and prove those naysayers wrong, was to provide humanity with the ability to control that which was responsible for all human suffering. Time itself. Time travel is of course widely theorised about and used throughout literature and media as an ability beyond ordinary human capabilities. So, what better way to achieve my dream, and become a god amongst men, than to harness the very essence of our universe and bend it to my will. It mattered little to me that my natural strength lay in biology and not physics, I had set my sights upon this goal, I would become the Godfather of Time Travel.

I of course achieved my ambition, which I'm sure gave Oscar Wilde a good chuckle, and at first it wasn't so bad, or at least there was nothing that could be construed as going immediately wrong. You see the problem with creating a 'time machine' as it were, is that the machine is useless until it ages. It's like a fine, aged, vintage wine or a beautiful, aromatic, mature cheese. I didn't so much as defy the rules of the universe, as find a loophole. The machine can only move from the point in time it currently exists, to back as far as the moment it was created.

As an example, the first working time machine was created on the 22nd of June 1967, and therefore the version of that time machine that exists today could only travel as far back as 22nd of June 1967. Conversely, the machine cannot travel to a moment in which it has not yet existed. In addition, the machine must always remain parallel to what I termed 'true time'. For instance, if the machine was in the past for two hours, fourteen minutes and thirty-eight seconds it must return two hours, fourteen minutes, and thirty-eight seconds after it left its 'true time' line. I suppose it might be easier to think of it like splicing a roll of film, if you imagine every single moment as a frame, you cannot reduce the length of the full tape roll, but you could change the order in which the frames are shown.

Zinc Anode

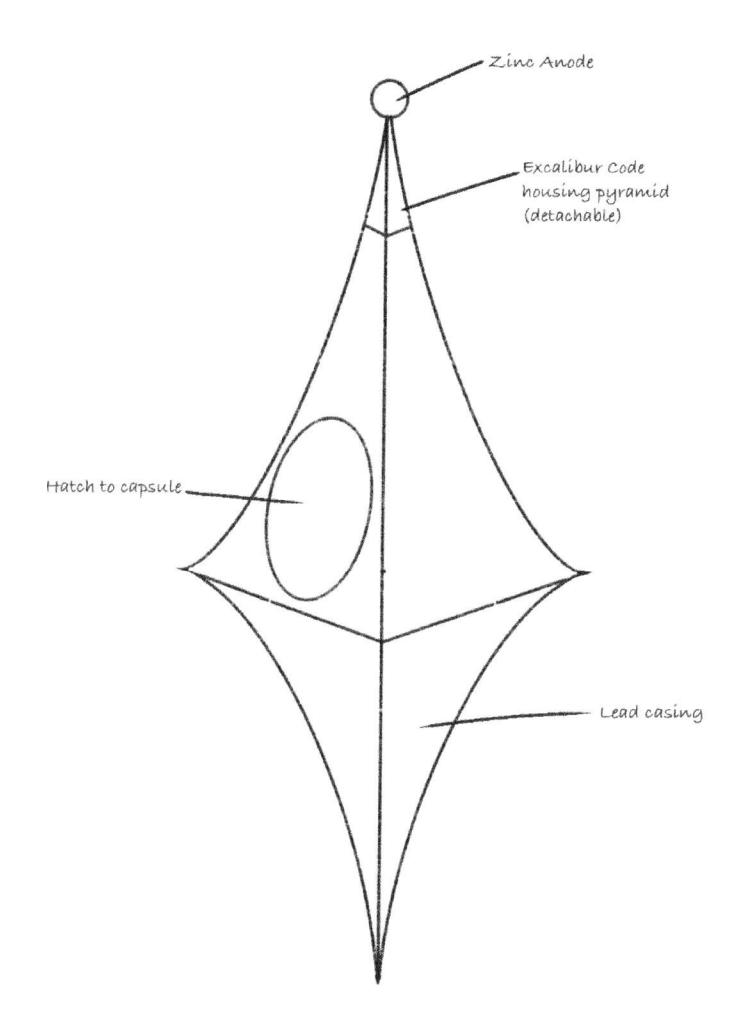

Excalibur Code
housing pyramid
(detachable)

Hatch to capsule

Lead casing

I have always enjoyed metaphors, this human art of speech where we masquerade something as something else, in the hopes that others will accept this mistruth.

Or perhaps they will see through our deception and will smile that sharp knowing smile of recognition.

I used a metaphor when I came to the grandiose business of naming my invention, you see I couldn't describe it as what it was:

The
Heretical
Engine that
Could
Literally be
A
Weapon

Besides it didn't look anything like a claw, so I came up with an acceptable metaphor to please my investors and inspire their faith in me and my work. For your appreciation:

Capsule for
Amelioration of
Life
Implementing
Guidance and
Order

Thus, the C.A.L.I.G.O device was duly christened. It was perhaps a little on the nose, and the big brother references shone through rather strongly, but

C.A.L.I.G.O was Latin in its origin, and I've found if you throw enough supposed culture at something, most people won't care what the truth is.

Looking back now, the biggest mistake I made in the genesis of the C.A.L.I.G.O device was how it was funded. To build a machine like that was a huge undertaking, and not one that could be made by a young man such as I; born to poor immigrant parents in South London far from riches, shortly after the outbreak of World War Two. I have often considered whether it was this upbringing that inspired my all-consuming desire to be a god amongst my peers. Perhaps the helplessness I felt in the face of the destruction mankind could willingly unleash upon itself in the name of war, inspired my need to control the very measurement of our lives.

My intentions for the C.A.L.I.G.O device's use, were ultimately for the good of humanity, for the prevention of disasters and wars, such as those I had experienced as a small child. To stop the suffering that clung to our species ever since Pandora opened her box. This, I suppose was too idealistic, as not everybody's idea of ameliorating life extended beyond their own interests. So, to begin the build of my device a deal was struck with a wealthy politician in her majesty's government, who I believe at the time held the title of Minister of Defence, he promised to fund every single part of the project. The only thing he asked for in return was that the device, if functional, was to be for the sole use of

Britain and its Government, I was also required to sign an agreement that made it an act of treason for me to ever divulge the existence of my device.

This went rather against my dreams of universal acclaim and worship. After all, if the world did not know of the existence of C.A.L.I.G.O how was I supposed to get my deserved reward? My hesitance was dispelled however, as this politician warned me of how others may consider my device a weapon and I could unwittingly throw the world into its next war. I certainly did not want history to remember me as the villain. So, in the throes of my fear I signed the papers and set to work.

The saying money is the root of all evil was far truer than I ever imagined, as this outwardly kindly politician who treated my theories with respect and listened to my far-out ramblings as though I spoke of something of importance, was perhaps the closest I have ever come to meeting the devil's own prophet. I imagine it was one of the easiest temptations he had ever accomplished. I was young and prideful and had been scorned for my outlandish ideas by my fellow physicists, I was so desperate, and he was so understanding of my troubles and eccentricities you see. I was played like the fool I was, and now you must suffer for my stupidity.

My deepest apologies

Anon.

Chapter 1

Michael Brown was distinctly odd, in the way that there was nothing at all remarkable about him. For most people who looked at him their gaze simply drifted to the side, as if their eyes could not comprehend something so uninteresting. He had dulled blond hair, that lay flat on his head, and muted grey-blue eyes. He dressed in a cool grey shirt, that almost matched his eyes, and black formal trousers. He was extremely unimpressive, and it wasn't just his appearance that was unexciting, but his personality felt stunted as though at some point it had just stopped developing. Nobody had ever seen Michael display anything other than bland, practiced happiness, slight sadness or complete neutrality, it was like anything more complex was simply beyond his understanding.

The truth was that Michael's personality had stopped developing at age ten. It had been frozen, put on hold, to be revisited at a time when Michael was free from his obligations. So, Michael's favourite song remained 'Thunderstruck' by AC/DC, which he'd heard on Top of the Pops a few days before his birthday. His favourite footballer was still Gordon Hill, and he remained without any of the emotional maturity and development he should have undergone in the following fifteen years.

On his tenth birthday he'd received a strange gift from a strange man, that foretold and detailed his life for the next fifteen years. It was a small black book with dates and instructions, written in what would come to be his own handwriting. It told the young boy of how if he followed these instructions, he would prevent the collapse of reality, by saving the life of the most important man who ever lived. At the time he first read the book, he had no idea who Professor Elijah Ainsley was, or why Ainsley's survival was so important as to warrant Michael giving up the remainder of his childhood. It was only later that Michael discovered that Professor Ainsley was the Godfather of Time Travel, and that if he failed in his mission, the universe would be torn apart by the paradox it would cause. For if Ainsley was killed before Time Travel was invented, then how could his assassin travel in time to kill him?

In the face of such momentous information, Michael did what any impressionable young child would do when told their actions could save the universe, he promised himself he would follow the book. He would save the life of the mysterious Professor Ainsley, and maybe become a tiny bit of a hero in the process. With such an enticing reward, Michael followed the books instructions to the letter, and put any and all choices that weren't decided by the book on hold.

So, here he was almost fifteen years later, only a day left on his clock, having followed every instruction to the letter. When without warning the Ministry had been exposed for unethical actions, and the miraculous time travel device itself lay powered down behind firmly padlocked doors. Leaving Michael reeling in the face of his uncertain future.

Michael checked his watch. He still had a few hours to wait until the assassin arrived. Not that he knew how the man intended to escape to the past, what with the C.A.L.I.G.O device sitting useless and impossible to get to in the Ministry that was currently on Red Alert. That didn't mean that the black book was wrong though. At least Michael hoped it didn't. There had to be some explanation for why his book had not warned him about this turn of events. Of course, there had been instances before when the book had neglected to mention something but nothing of this scale. He drummed his fingers on the steel table. The digits itched in what Michael had come to recognise was a nervous need to hold his book. Even though logically he knew it was only some words in a small pocketbook, it was his whole life, it was his reassurance and guarantee that everything was planned out for him and all he had to do was follow it.

"What'd you reckon then?" Came the voice of one of the few other people with a northern accent. Michael looked up to see Mark Stobbs, a fellow technician, stood next to him. He was a stick thin man who wore baggy creased clothes at least one size too big for him. Mark was of short stature with the posture of a man used to stooping through doorways, an ironic image. His eyes were sharp and clever like the rest of his features, and he had a smile that curled with an air of mischief. Stobbs was generally disliked by most of the divisions and upper-level staff, as he wasn't too fond of authority or doing things simply because someone told him to. Yet despite their dislike, Mark had a way of wheedling what he wanted out of their superiors. He was notoriously late and rude and yet there was not a single black mark against his name. He never ceased to baffle Michael. However, what confused him perhaps the most was why Mark bothered with him. Mark was witty and charming, that is if he wanted to be, and could do much better for a conversation partner than Michael Brown.

"What do I reckon about what?" Michael asked genially.
"The news you muppet!" He said as though Michael was being deliberately obtuse, and ruffled Michael's hair before taking the seat opposite him.
"I don't know." Michael replied honestly. He didn't really think he was qualified to have an opinion on it, he was not someone in charge of making those unethical decisions, but he also hadn't been affected, as far as he knew, by those decisions. Stobbs smiled as though

Michael had said something particularly funny, but also completely expected. Mark was the only Ministry employee who saw Michael as an actual person, and seemed to find his lack of opinions amusing, like it was a deliberately cultivated aspect of Michael's personality. He was strange like that.

"You never know much of anything." He pointed out, adopting a long-suffering tone.
"Well, what do you think then?" Michael asked. Stobbs grinned, mischievous.
"I reckon it were Ainsley hisself!" Michael laughed at that; Mark could always be trusted to come out with the most ridiculous statements.
"You think the great inventor would expose the Ministry? After he created them, and the C.A.L.I.G.O device?" Michael shook his head vehemently. "No way! Ainsley has had barely anything to do with us in decades and has only had about four public appearances in that time!" Stobbs grinned wider, triumphant.

"See you do have an opinion!" Stobbs exclaimed triumphantly. Michael regarded him, confused.
"What do you mean?" Michael questioned, entirely exasperated by the whole conversation.
"You always have an opinion, where Elijah's involved. Sure a way as any to get an answer out of you, insult our resplendent lord and saviour." Michael sighed, talking with Mark was like conversing in circles with a man who hoped you'd go insane before the end of the

conversation, but at least the ache in his fingers had dulled.

"How's Harry?" Mark changed the subject. Michael looked over to where his brother sat with the other members of A Division around a table examining the examples of exposed documents on a computer.
"He's okay, I think. I mean he's Harry, he's always good in a crisis." Michael answered, entirely unsure of what he was supposed to say to that. Harry Brown was the brilliant Executor of A Division, he was the poster boy for the Ministry's success, as far as anyone could be a poster boy for a secret organisation, and Michael's older brother. There was very little similarity in the two men, Harry was well known and adored amongst their Ministry colleagues while Michael was never seen as much more than an afterthought. His brother had shining gold hair, a charming smile and he oozed confidence, a sharp contrast to Michael. Harry had always been the overachiever when they were kids, always smart, always kind, and always the hero. They had a very underdeveloped brotherly relationship, which Michael knew was his fault. He respected his brother and was proud of his achievements and he hoped when his quest was over, they could be proper brothers. As they always should have been.

"Yeah, I know, he could fall in a load of sheep shit and come up smelling of roses." Mark said quite viciously. Mark seemed to have adopted the anger he thought

Michael should harbour against his brother but didn't. "You don't have to pretend with me Michael, you can say he's a git." Stobbs implored as though Michael was holding out on him.
"I don't think that." Michael responded honestly.
"Then you're an idiot. He swans about like he owns the place, all cos he's the great Executor of A Division, the darling of the Ministry. As good as Lizzie Jones, who we all know was the greatest Agent to have ever graced these hallowed halls." Michael raised his eyebrows at the excess sarcasm. "And yet he treats his own brother like a second-class citizen. I swear I'm the only person round here who even remembers you even exist."
"It's fine." Michael said placatingly.
"It's not, and one day you're gonna realise it, and when you do, I'm gonna be there for you." Mark promised solemnly.

"So go on then, who do you think is really behind all these unethical changes?" Michael tried to drag the conversation away from topics that would stoke Mark's anger.
"Politicians innit?" Mark responded, his earlier enthusiasm had clearly dissipated. Michael sighed; he was rubbish at this. Conversations were always difficult, he never knew quite what to say, mainly because he didn't really have an opinion on anything. He was happy to be invited into conversation as long as the other person didn't expect too much from him. With Mark he never had to worry about starting conversation, the

other Mancunian could talk for England and Michael didn't have to worry about giving disappointing answers.

"But why?" Michael tried again. Mark huffed a laugh.

"Money and Power what else?" The other technician replied. "I'm not surprised. They've probably had their grubby hands all over our history since C.A.L.I.G.O was invented." He took another breath to say something else when the canteen doors slammed open.

September 30th, 1972

The C.A.L.I.G.O device is a miracle, and while it was a challenge to develop the project as a whole, the real difficulty of the matter was sustaining life through time travel. It is fairly simple to send an inanimate object back through its own time stream. After all, objects don't have a tendency to move by themselves, unless acted upon by an external force as Newton so elegantly observed. Therefore, there are, to return my earlier metaphor, many frames in the film reel of the object existing at this point in time and space, and it is rather simple to select the correct one you wish to return the object to. It is different for living beings, our homeostasis is constantly changing every microsecond, and we don't have the decency to remain in one place, unchanging for vast amounts of time. This poses a problem, as to send a being back in time would return you to how and where you were at that moment, so perhaps you would end up three years old in a house that no longer exists, and your heart would freeze in that frame, unable to handle the conflicting messages from your body.

Naturally, I was able to remedy this issue, instead of moving time through the object or being as would be the easiest method, you needed the universe to accept the presence of beings and objects that shouldn't necessarily be present. I had to find a way to temporarily suspend the universal rules allowing the incongruous presence of my device and its inhabitants.

To allow the sustainability of life, and ensure synchronicity, The Excalibur Code was developed, it creates a small loop in the flow of time thereby not disrupting an individual's forward flowing timeline but allowing them to return to a moment earlier in the universe's own timeline. It is ingenious, I am well aware. Without the Excalibur Code, time moves through the object and not the other way around, and any life that attempted to travel with it would perish. This is because the universe would recognise you were in the wrong place at the wrong time, and it would extinguish you, so that it would not lose itself.

The code has never been read by anyone but its creator. I have heard some more simple-minded individuals say, that it is because to look upon such a creation is to stare at a secret of the universe, and it would send any man insane to have such knowledge. This is foolish. I am the only person to have seen the code because I have made it so. If others saw the code, the C.A.L.I.G.O device could be replicated by lesser men, and its power misused. I have no desire to set another monster free upon this world. I will not allow the same mistake to be made twice. I am better than my fellow men.

The Ministry of Time was created to look after the C.A.L.I.G.O device, and ensure its proper use, of course occasionally the device will break down and suffer problems like any other technology. For this reason, there are specially trained technicians trusted to repair the device, the first of which I trained personally. However, the Excalibur Code remains guarded by me, and my refusal to hand it over, leaves the Ministry terrified of me. It is my leverage over them, my trump card. I know the nature of man and I knew there was a strong possibility that once I had outlived my usefulness I would be cut loose, and my device taken from me to be used as they saw fit. The thing about power is that once men have it, they do not want to let go, much less share it, and so I ensured I would always have a hand on the wheel, a finger on the button, a seat at the table.

It has not taken long for my relationship with the Ministry to go sour, I have been relegated to a minor member on the Ethics Committee, where my voice is ignored. So, I am suspended in this power struggle. I have my hands on another wheel though. One the ministry is unaware of.

   People are always the pitfall of any large organisation, and the Ministry of Time is no different. You see their mistake is training agents to blindly follow that which is inscribed upon a black book. Black books are holy grails to agents. They contain instructions and time markers for agents, informing them how they completed their missions the first time they did so. Instructions written in their own hand by some future version of themselves. It is in the nature of humanity to rebel against orders given by a faceless authority, but instructions given by ourselves? Of course, we will follow those, its only like following a voice in your own head after all.

   Alison Thomas is not as I remembered her. She is much younger. She sits sipping coffee, reading a book a few tables over from me. In my pocket her black book lies; it is strange to be parting with it after I have held it for five years. I stand up, keeping my head low and my hat covering as much as my face as possible. I stride towards her table and clasp the black book in my gloved hand. As I pass her by, I slide it on to her table and move quickly away, vanishing into the crowd outside the shop.

   It is a strange feeling to change the course of someone's life, it is a forbidden power but one I have used twice already this morning, now three times. I have *set their lives on a selfish course, to seek my own ends, but it must be done, as it has already happened for me and so it must happen for them.*

E.

Chapter 2

A few hours after the news broke, the police had finally stormed the Ministry of Time and were holding all employees for interviewing. Michael surreptitiously checked his watch, there was only an hour and a half until Professor Ainsley's assassin would steal the C.A.L.I.G.O device, and the entire Ministry building was on red alert. No one could even move from their seat without a heavily armed officer asking who they were, and where they thought they were going. Michael could feel the hard suspicious gazes that swept the room, as they decided who they were going to pull in next. Fortunately for the police, the Ministry had interview and interrogation rooms in the building, owing to the high level of confidentiality that had been an essential requirement for working there. Mark was still seated opposite him; he was full of some restless energy and his eyes snapped to anyone who moved. "Have you noticed that only some of the staff are coming back from these interviews?" He whispered to Michael.

It was true, and Michael himself had noticed that only about ten percent of those they tapped for interrogation returned to the canteen.

"Maybe they're letting the others go home for the moment, if they don't know anything of relevance?" Michael theorised.

"Nothing of relevance? All of its bloody relevant! The world has just been told that time travel exists, and they think some parts just aren't relevant?" Mark hissed back at him.

"Well yeah, but only some of it is actually criminal by today's laws."

"That's because there are no laws about Time Travel." Mark pointed out.

"Exactly, so most of it can't be judged as having been illegal. At the moment the only thing they can really arrest for, is imposing upon human rights and stuff to do with civil service agreements." Mark rolled his eyes and began drumming his fingers.

"But how much is immoral? We changed the course of history, and yeah it might have been better for some, but worse for others. How do you judge the moral weight of what we did?"

"That's for more important people than me to decide."

Half an hour had passed, and Michael found himself checking his watch with every passing minute. He needed to get out of this room. "Got somewhere to be?" Mark asked after Michael looked at the time to see only thirty seconds had passed since he'd last looked.

"No." He replied immediately. He'd learnt early on that telling others about the black book only got him ridiculed and dismissed, even in the institution where black books were commonplace, they were not meant for the likes of Michael Brown. Black books were agent accounts from a future version of themselves that were issued by the Collators office at the correct point in their own timeline for them to then go back and complete it. After the agents completed their mission, they would hand the black book back into the Collators at that earlier point in time, so that it could be reissued to them again in the future. As a technician Michael should never have even come into contact with a black book and yet perhaps the most important black book ever written belonged to him. His future. His mission. His heroic ending.

"Could've fooled me. You must have checked your watch twenty times over the last ten minutes." Michael shrugged.

"Just wondering when we get to go home." Mark scoffed but dropped the subject.

Another ten minutes passed before Michael looked up to see Harry being returned to the canteen. He frowned at the sight, surely Harry had not been a part of the unethical missions? Mark turned around to look and smiled at the sight. "See, I told you he wasn't as squeaky clean as he pretends. I knew there was no way you get to be the Director's personal favourite without having got your hands dirty. Wonder what he got from it?

Probably a pay rise, or some other juicy benefit, although he could have done it just to be the golden boy, which just makes it worse of course." Michael ignored his friends' scorn and watched his brother, as his own team moved further down their table to get away from him. Dire times were afoot when an Accountant abandoned their Executor.

Michael looked up as an armed policeman tapped his shoulder. "Michael Brown." His gruff voice permeated through his visor. The officer wore a heavy stab vest and was armed with a handgun that was strapped to his side. A snood mask covered his nose and mouth. He practically loomed over Michael who had suddenly never felt smaller. It sounded more like a statement than a question, but Michael responded all the same. "Yes."
"Come with me." Michael slid out from underneath the table and straightened his shirt; he walked beside the man down the canteen. Harry looked up as he passed, with something like anxiety etched across his face. Michael was led down the bare corridors of the Ministry, they were dark, grey, and claustrophobic. Even if you knew the way, déjà vu screamed painfully at your senses crying that you were walking in circles. Michael shivered reflexively and was suddenly glad of the policeman beside him, for the sign of life.

His armed officer took him roughly by the elbow and forced him to a stop outside a nondescript battleship grey door. Michael was unreasonably nervous and not just because of what could be behind the door. Time was slipping away from him. The assassin would make his move soon and Michael was trapped. His guarding officer rapped twice on the heavy metal door before opening it and leading Michael into the room beyond.

There was a suited woman sat across from him at a metal table and a spare chair in front of Michael. He heard the officer leave and the door slam shut behind him causing him to jump. Every sense in Michael's body seemed to be on edge as he was locked into the interrogation room. To his left the only disruption to the blank walls was a large pane of one-way glass that caused an unpleasant feeling to curl down his spine as if he could suddenly feel a thousand eyes watching him.

"Please sit down." She gestured to the available chair, before turning back to the large collection of pages and documents in front of her. Michael did as she asked, wincing as the chair scraped against the linoleum floor, and waited for her to address him further. Her blonde hair was neatly slicked back into a bun and scrutinising blue eyes perused the documents in front of her. She had an air of frightening professionalism and was effortlessly intimidating.

"Do you want a lawyer?" She asked after a moment, still not looking up from the files. She seemed almost bored as she asked the question.

"I didn't know we were being given lawyers?"
"You aren't, but so far everyone has demanded one the moment they entered this room." She explained turning her dissecting gaze on him and lacing her fingers together, before resting them on the piles of pages. She fixed him with that piercing look as though hoping to pluck the secrets of the Ministry of Time from his mind without words.

"I don't have anything to hide." Michael replied honestly, he just needed this to be over as soon as possible. She nodded in what seemed like amused disbelief and looked down at her notepad.
"You're Harry Brown's brother, yes?" She started with.
"I am." Michael confirmed.
"So, you're aware of the missions he has taken part in?" She said almost rhetorically, raising her pen in preparation for his answer.
"No, not really." She looked back up at him in surprise. "Harry and I aren't that close, and I'm part of B Division anyway so we don't work together." She noted something down and regarded him anew.
"But you know the missions that have been completed by the field team at B Division." She tried again, her gaze assessing him once again.
"No sorry. The details become fuzzy after a while, something to do with the conflicting versions of timelines." Michael shrugged his shoulders in what he imagined came across as apologetic uselessness.

"But you worked on those missions?" She asked incredulous, unfortunately her tone told Michael he'd instead piqued her interest.

"I did, but everyone's memories get changed after the C.A.L.I.G.O device returns. I remember what I did at work, and the people I worked with, but I can never really recall what part of history was changed, or what originally happened." He explained trying to make himself appear as useless as possible.
"So, as a Technician you are just like the general public? Your memories are not preserved?" She began to piece it together. Michael began to get the unfortunate feeling that in fact no one else had been telling them anything and Michael's unlikely compliance was a gold mine for them.

"Yes, the only people who remember their missions are the field team, and Historians have to be briefed once a week about what has changed, if they were not a part of the mission themselves." She gave a small smile and scribbled down what he had said.
"Do you know why that is?" She enquired.
"No, no one does." She ticked her head in confusion.
"I thought you were a technician?" The way she said it, it was like she'd caught him out.
"I am, but much of the C.A.L.I.G.O device and its functioning is unknown. Only its creator will have those answers."

"Professor Elijah Ainsley?" There was a strange quality to her voice as she asked him.

"Yeah." He confirmed, unpleasant realisation tickling his mind.

"So, Ainsley didn't tell the Ministry everything about the device?"

"No." With that the woman looked towards the one-way glass and nodded.

Chapter 3

Michael heard the door open behind him and a young man in a sharp suit appeared. He was clean shaven, with perfectly coiffed hair and a pristine black suit. He exuded power, charisma, and the sticky unpleasant feeling of deceit. Suddenly staying in Michael's interrogation room felt positively cosy and homely against the prospect of going with that man.

"Why don't you come with us Mr Brown?" He smiled falsely and Michael felt entirely uneasy, but he stood up and made his way out of the door as instructed. In the hall, three others stood waiting for him, an older gentleman dressed in an expensive suit who to Michael's relief did not seem to be part of the secret service. A young woman in a maintenance jumpsuit accompanied him, looking entirely out of place amongst her smartly dressed colleagues; and the armed policeman from earlier stood behind them, likely as a group escort.

The young man clapped a hand on Michael's shoulder. "We wondered if you might show us the C.A.L.I.G.O device?" His tone made it clear it was not optional, but Michael nodded all the same. At least he was going in the direction he wanted to be, but now he had little idea of what time was left until the assassin would make an appearance. The younger man kept his hand on Michael's shoulder as he steered him through the corridors. The finely dressed gentleman and the young woman followed behind them, while the officer brought up the rear. Eventually, they arrived at the chained double doors that lead into the affectionately named 'Time Hall'. Michael was surprised there was no 'Keep Out' sign posted on the doors, but then the industrial chain wrapped around the handles with its large padlock holding them together conveyed the message on its own.

Finally, the man took his heavy hand off Michael's shoulder and reached into his pocket to produce a key. Michael rolled his shoulders to try and release the ache and phantom weight the man had put there but was unsuccessful. The padlock clicked its release, the large chain rattled and clanked as it was unwound. It looked like they were trying to keep something inside, rather than keep anyone out. Eventually, the man pushed the two doors open and his entourage entered behind him.

Michael looked up at the majesty that was the C.A.L.I.G.O device. Every time he laid his eyes on it, it never ceased to leave him breathless. It was a magnificent amalgamation of technology and impossibility. It was proof of humanity's accomplishments and understanding of the universe around them. It stood at a massive ten metres tall and five metres diameter, it was perfectly symmetrical and seemed without seam or imperfection. To stand in its presence was to look at something more than even the most cutting edge of technology. It was an elongated octahedron, a shape used for crystals and precious stones, a shape used for beauty. Its lead casing made it grey to the untrained eye, but there was also a blue hue that shone through which granted an ethereal look to the device. It stood on its lowest point like an impossible, immoveable monument. It was simply beautiful. He cast a glance to the side where it seemed his company was in a similar state of awe as they took in the sight.

It was strange to stand in the room without the usual hum of instruments or the flashing lights. "When you're ready Mr Brown." The gentleman in his finery invited, his booming voice laced with culture. Michael looked between them and grappled for somewhere to begin. How do you explain the C.A.L.I.G.O device? It was more than a mechanical device, it was an idea, a phenomenon, an abstract culmination of humanity's hopes and innovation.

Maybe it was best to start simple rather than try and explain the nature of time and space Michael thought. "Alright, well over in the insulated cage is the control centre, which monitors the levels of energy, fuel and potential in the C.A.L.I.G.O device." He pointed to the crow's nest. "The device won't travel unless all measurements are exact, as a health precaution. Too much energy and you could risk losing the device in Time, too little it could strand its passengers at a random point in time and not take them home." He explained, the three of them nodded their understanding as their guard remained motionless.

"C.A.L.I.G.O has an accuracy of plus or minus three minutes and forty-one seconds from the moment you set it to arrive at. It receives energy from the copper cathode on top of the control centre, which travels to the zinc anode atop the device itself. The outer layer is lead, to protect its occupants from the electromagnetic waves that are generated by the journey. There is a round hatch that provides access to the capsule; and in the small pyramid attachment at the tip of the device the 'Excalibur code' is housed." Michael had led them over to the stairs up to the viewing gangplank.
"What's the Excalibur code?" The young woman asked as she regarded in turn, each part of the device that Michael had pointed out.

"It allows life to be sustained inside the C.A.L.I.G.O device, but also ensures that its occupants are not affected by the movement in time, and their current homeostasis is maintained throughout their travel until they are returned to their proper place in their own timeline." He led them up the stairs, their heavy footfalls echoing throughout the quiet, empty chamber.

"When the device travels back in time where does it end up? Surely not here?" The older gentleman asked.
"No, there is another chamber similar to this one that has two docks. It's called the 'Half-Way' Hall." Michael explained pointing vaguely beyond the far wall of the chamber where the mirrored hall was supposed to be. He had never been there himself, only agents had ever seen or been inside the Half-Way Hall.
"Why two docks?" The woman put in.
"In case anything goes wrong. Another future version of the C.A.L.I.G.O device could travel back and correct any issue. Though if anything goes wrong after that nothing can be done about it, as there's nowhere for C.A.L.I.G.O to land. It becomes what we have termed 'fixed' time, as it can no longer be changed."

Michael opened the access hatch before pausing and looking to the young man. "Can I get in the capsule?" He asked. The young man smiled, seemingly enjoying Michael's deference to him.
"Of course, just keep the hatch open." Michael nodded his understanding and stepped down into the capsule.

He crouched down by the small control panel. When he looked back to his audience the young man had disappeared, not that Michael was in a position to query where he had gone, but still it left him more than a little uneasy.
"This is where the destination is programmed by the field team." He gestured to the small keypad of numbers. Michael didn't really understand why they had asked him to do this, he was by no means the most experienced technician, and all he was telling them was in the manuals that they had surely read.

His demonstration soon stopped however when the device roared to life beneath his feet. He looked up panicked to see equal shock on the faces of the young woman and the older man. "Step away from the device." Came the cool voice of the young man, he held a handgun pointed at the two civilians. They raised their hands, and followed the man's instructions as he guided them down the gangplank. Michael waited frozen in the device, but as the man disappeared, he quickly moved over to the Accountant's chair in the far-left corner. Under the seat a spare gun was stored in case of emergencies. He unclipped it and tucked it in the back of his trousers, his hands shook with adrenaline and shock, but he faced the hatch and kept quiet. At least he no longer had to worry about being late. It seemed he was right on time.

He heard the metal clanging of industrial boots against the metal walkway and to Michael's surprise the officer advanced towards the C.A.L.I.G.O device, with his own handgun drawn at his side. His face was still covered as his eyes bored into Michael's, cold and determined. In the background, Michael could make out the young man's profile in the crow's nest. How had they got the device running? Most of the Ministry was powered down and there was almost certainly a circuit breaker in place between the generators and the device. The officer stepped into the device, keeping his gun pointed squarely at Michael's chest. The hatch hissed closed behind him. Michael swallowed against his dry throat trying to calm himself by the feel of the gun against his lower back. "Don't move." The same gruff voice from the canteen told him.

"Who are you?" Michael asked, he knew what was going to happen. He had been preparing for this moment his whole life. What reason was there to be scared? When he had spent his whole life waiting for this moment right now. His hands shook regardless of his assurances.
"Shut up." The man told him abruptly, before turning his back to Michael and pressing buttons on the keypad. Michael saw his chance and drew his gun aiming for the man's back.
"Stop." He commanded, as his hand gripped the cool metal of the weapon tightly; his heart was thumping

hard in his chest at a million miles an hour, he hadn't expected how real this was going to feel.

The man stopped for a moment, before snapping his arm around, catching hold of Michael's own and throwing him to the side against the device wall. Pain flared up his left flank, but he kept a hold of his weapon. The man hit the enter key and pulled the engage lever. The device gave an almighty shudder and Michael almost fell to the floor with the force of C.A.L.I.G.O setting off. He went to raise his gun arm again, but the masquerading policeman slammed his fist into Michael's stomach, and he doubled over in pain.

"I knew you'd be here Michael. Such a good little soldier." The assassin spat with the venom of a man who knew true hatred. "You should know that the book is lying to you. Everyone is lying to you." Something cold and heavy made itself home in his stomach as the assassin spoke. "I should kill you now. You'd thank me for it, if you knew what was coming," Michael stumbled amidst the rattling of the device, and he tried once again to raise his gun against his enemy, but the man caught his arm with ease and yanked the weapon from his hands.

Michael could hear his blood roar in his ears as his mind only repeated one thing, that this was not going how it was supposed to. "But I think someone else should understand. You will understand Michael, and then you will die miserable and alone." He reached behind him and pulled the lever again; the C.A.L.I.G.O device gave a great heave in protest, and it shuddered to a halt. The hatch behind him hissed open, and the masked assassin reached forward and pushed him hard out the door.

Michael stumbled back over the lip of the device and reached out, trying to catch the railings to his side, but they were too wide, and he found himself tipping over the edge of the stairs. His head cracked against metal, and his final vision was of the C.A.L.I.G.O device sealing shut without him before everything went dark.

April 9th, 1975

For every monster there must be someone holding the leash, and for my device and me the leash was held by the Ministry of Time. They sound like a perfectly respectable division of government, trustworthy, benevolent, and powerful. Unfortunately, only one of those adjectives is actually applicable, and I can confirm that it's not one of the two that you would hope for.

Originally, they were set up as a subdivision of the Ministry of Defence, and the first Time Agents were promising transfers from MI6. Although, as missions began to take place, it became clear that being able to fire a gun to the usual standard requirements of espionage, was not sufficient to ensure the success of potential time travel missions. Having, what the Ministry of Time tentatively called, my mysterious foresight, I had made sure there was enough space for four potential members of a field team on the C.A.L.I.G.O device. They experimented with several configurations, before settling upon an Executor, an Accountant, a Chameleon, and a Historian.

The Executor is the principal agent, and has the final say on all operational matters, once aboard the C.A.L.I.G.O device. They of course, carry a state issued firearm and remain the least unspecialised of agents from the original MI6 crop. The Accountant functions as a second to the Executor, they are capable of calculating up to a certain point, the impact of actions taken by field agents upon the flow of time. They tend to be stuffy, exacting and lacking a sense of humour, much like their namesake in the field of finance.

Historians work closely with Accountants, and in my opinion remain the most powerful and unyielding of agents. Each week they are taken down to the Collator's office and return knowing the flow of 'true time' including that which has been changed. They advise their fellow team members of the time they are in, including any other missions that took place at a similar time, to prevent clashes or interference. Another one of their duties, is to sit on the Ethics Committee, which was a strategic move by the Ministry of Time to reduce the amount of people who have knowledge of discrepancies in the flow of time. To those more cynical, this also cleverly reduced the number of independent voices on the Ethics Committee.

Chameleons are another special type of agent; one I had a hand in creating. They are trained in the art of blending in. I do not mean this in the simple sense of not being noticed, but rather being noticed for the right reasons. They are skilled in the production of fake documents and identifications, but also in disguising their fellow agents as important people in history. It is not a fine art and would not be able to fool those who knew the target particularly well, but it would be enough to get past certain securities or at least a short conversation with those who knew them reasonably well.

There are three divisions consisting of these four agents plus a team of technicians and an individual termed 'The Guv'. The Governor exists as the authority inside the Time Hall. They engage the C.A.L.I.G.O device and make all final calls. These three divisions are A, B, and C and each have eight hour shifts each day ensuring there is always a team with C.A.L.I.G.O twenty-four hours a day.

The four specialised agents make up a field team in the Ministry of Time and carry out the missions, but they are not the Ministry's crowning glory. As a result of the missions, the Collator's office is aware of future events, they know when to issue black books to agents at the correct point in their lifetime, and therefore they know future events and changes. It is this way because otherwise the paradoxes would collapse in on themselves, and the laws of the universe would be broken rather than carefully subverted, as I have so masterfully accomplished.

It may seem unbelievable, but I knew the burden of knowledge that I would be handing to the Ministry. I knew I would give them the answers to the future. I knew there would be a special few who would understand the universe's forbidden will of the future. I trusted that these individuals would be like me, silent guardians over the truth, that they would have the best interests of humanity in mind in their privileged position. Yet, I understood that they could not be the only safeguard.

The Ethics Committee was my final gift to the Ministry of Time, my final godly protection I provided them. A way to be sure they were working in the interests of the majority, and not themselves. Strange, how I now find myself an outsider upon a committee I set up. They glare at me as though I were a leper among them, rather than the only god willing to share in his fortune, failing to recognise the man who made them the people they are today.

The only reason I can find for their hatred against me is that someone is poisoning the well against me. Perhaps in their knowledge of the future they see me as a threat. I am sure the Ministry is behind it, and it causes me to worry. If they are capable of making the Ethics Committee unethical, perhaps I have misjudged their readiness for me and my creation. I fear I have made a great mistake in trusting in the basic goodness in people. It is clear now that their fear of me is larger than I first acknowledged, and they hope to force me out sooner rather than later.

Elijah

Chapter 4

The first thing Michael was aware of was that his head hurt, a lot. It felt like someone was trying to drive an ice pick into his skull. He groaned in pain and tried to raise his right hand to examine what had happened to his head, only to be stopped by a tight metal cuff against his wrist, keeping his arm in place. Confused and rather dazed, he opened his eyes to a bleary ceiling that was not familiar. It smelt of TCP and antiseptics; it was also very bright and sterile, which did not help his headache. He tried to recall what had happened to him but drew a complete blank.

"Are you awake?" Came a clear male voice from somewhere to his right. It caused the hammer knocking against his forehead to strike harder, and he groaned petulantly. "Michael, can you look at me?" Slowly, Michael tilted his head in the direction of the voice, to gaze blearily at the face of a man in his late forties with prominent sideburns and half rimmed spectacles. He wore a white doctors coat over a bland brown suit. Clearly, he was unaware that time had moved on since the eighties. "Excellent, now Michael what's your full name?"

"Michael James Brown." Michael replied sluggishly.

"Lovely. And when were you born?" The man, who Michael assumed was a Doctor, congratulated Michael's rather simple answer.

"September 27th, 1980." He managed.

"Very nice and how old are you?" Michael had to think on that one a moment before replying.

"Twenty-four."

"Not bad at all." The man announced to the room. "Now do you feel up to answering some more complex questions, Michael?"

"Sure," Michael attempted a shrug, but beyond the pain in his head he couldn't really feel any other part of his body, so he wasn't sure how that looked. The bed began to creak beneath him as it rearranged itself into an upright position, allowing Michael to see the rest of the room. To his right, ancient looking medical equipment was set up by his bed. The screens were clunky and made of beige plastic with thick black cords attaching them to the wall. Had they been severely underfunded? He blinked the light out of his eyes and squinted at the two other people shapes stood beside his bed.

At first, he only half recognised them, having only ever seen photos of them, and with his head like it was, he was not as quick as he should be. They were Elizabeth Jones and Christopher Stevens; the best Executor and Accountant the Ministry had ever produced. Their picture hung in the Collators' Office, with their names emblazoned on a gold plaque beneath it. Elizabeth was tall, and presented a powerful silhouette, as she matched the secret service standard of fitness. Her strawberry blonde hair was pulled back from her face in a militant style, with no single hair out of place. She had beautiful eyes that dissected and assessed all they fell upon. A large deep green military jacket covered her black shirt; she wore skintight dark blue jeans and black trainers.

Christopher, in contrast wore a perfectly tailored two-piece suit, that was a light grey to match his tie, and a pristine white shirt. He wore dress shoes; he had brown hair that looked almost black, which was swept off his face, and piercing eyes. It was an honour to meet them. Michael was about to tell them as much before Elizabeth spoke.

"Do you know what year it is?" She asked with what looked like slight hesitance. This made Michael pause. It had been 2005, but Jones and Stevens were not a part of the Ministry in 2005, and they certainly wouldn't be in their late twenties. The weird technology and the awful dress sense of the supposed doctor was another indication that perhaps Michael was not where he should be. Michael battled against the fog that hung over his mind, forcing himself to try and remember how he had gotten here. Half-formed images of an interrogation appeared in his mind. Then him crouching in the C.A.L.I.G.O device with a gun hidden in his trousers, as an armed officer who was not a real policeman, but was very much still armed, pointed a gun at him. The C.A.L.I.G.O device juddering through time; a battle for his gun which he lost; finally, the image of falling from the device, as its door closed behind him.

"No." Michael replied shakily, not at all looking forward to the answer.
"It's 1977." Said Christopher without intonation. Michael felt abruptly cold all over; he was stranded. Undoubtedly the 2005 C.A.L.I.G.O device had left without him, and he was now out of sync with it.

Could he still get home? Surely that's what Jones and Stevens were here for? They were here to give him the good news, that they had stopped the assassin and his

C.A.L.I.G.O device he had travelled in sat safe, and in sync with him in their Half-Way Hall.

"What were you doing in the C.A.L.I.G.O device?" Jones asked him. Michael forced himself to calm down and answer her question, for the sooner he did, the sooner he could go home.

"There was a man in there who was going to kill Professor Ainsley in 1967, before he could invent Time Travel." He managed, focussing on the facts.

"What do you remember about him?" Jones probed further. Michael forced some of the memories to become clearer and winced at the resulting pain in his head.

"He pretended to be a guard; when I was in the device, he and his accomplice started C.A.L.I.G.O up, and he forced his way inside." Michael answered haltingly. "When we were in motion there was a fight, he got a hold of my gun and threw me out. I don't remember much else." Stevens nodded and then held up the gun Michael had grabbed from under the seat.

"This your gun?" He asked.

"Yeah, that's it." Michael nodded, glad they were following his story, because his head made everything rather difficult. Stevens nodded in consideration before looking to his Executor.

"Where'd you get this?" Jones asked holding up his black book.

"I've had that since I was ten." Michael replied a little bewildered by the question.

"Really?" She said scepticism colouring her tone.
"Yes." Michael insisted. She raised an eyebrow and cast a glance to her second. Some sort of wordless conversation took place between the two agents before Elizabeth looked back to him.

"Here's what we think happened. You and Ainsley's assassin are in cahoots; and you stole this," she waved his black book, "from your brother, so that he would have no idea about the plot." Michael tried to keep up with the accusation as his head throbbed in time with his heartbeat. "Then mid mission, you and the assassin fell out and he dumped you here. Tell me I'm wrong." She laid out and Michael could only stare at her.

"You *are* wrong. I was given that book on my tenth birthday by a man in a long coat and sunglasses who thanked me for my service. I have followed every step in that book to ensure that I could stop Professor Ainsley's assassin. I gave up my whole life for that book!" He shouted at her, a strange something coursed through his blood at her words. Something long starved had awoken in his stomach, it clawed at his insides demanding action and pain. Was this what other people called rage? Michael wondered absently.

"Then how come you had a gun? If you had simply stepped into the C.A.L.I.G.O device with no knowledge that the guard was really Ainsley's assassin, you would not have been armed, you are only a technician after all." The Accountant put in. The creature snarled at the core of him, and Michael felt the fiery anger cut through the pain and haze of his mind, allowing a brief clarity.

"The gun was under the Accountant's seat, as has been standard practice for years! And if you'd bothered to read that book you claim I stole, you'd see that *it* told me to become a technician. And for your information, my brother is not a technician, nor has he ever been technically minded, he's an idiot with a gun! Like every other Executor." He threw in snidely hoping to drag Jones down into the fire with him.

It worked, and she stormed forward, throwing his book to her Accountant, and producing an identical one from her jacket pocket. She held it open on a page for him to see. "The Executor, Harry Brown from 2005, will arrive carrying the final black book, that will instruct you on how to save Elijah Ainsley." She read aloud for him. Michael felt like she had disembowelled him as he looked at his brother's name in her book. Surely not? Surely, he had not given up his whole life thus far for nothing? It had to be a joke. He was not his brother's poor replica, not now, not here. This was his chance to be Michael Brown not Harry Brown's brother. This had been his fate for fifteen years; what he was owed for his sacrifices. He could feel Jones' accusing gaze on him as she dared him to challenge her, but in contrast to the energy anger had given him, he now felt hollowed out, as though breathing alone took everything he had left.

In the distance, he could hear Stevens confirming what Michael had said about his book instructing him to become a technician. There was a further discussion between the two of them that Michael tuned out, maybe they tried to ask him another question, but he couldn't hear them, for he was drowning. Drowning in the endless questions that had taken the place of the sure statements he had comforted himself with for almost fifteen years. Emotions he had never felt before swarmed his mind and he could barely process what they were.

After a while they left, and his black book was placed at his bedside table beside his other meagre possessions. He only noticed later that his head had returned to its aching, but Michael could not bring enough focus to care.

March 3rd, 1978

I've always hated obituaries, they consist of a decidedly unremarkable couple of lies written by a small-time journalist, in some repurposed closet of the quiet office of a local rag, that will line cat litter boxes for the next week. For most people, it is perhaps the only time their name appears in the paper, and unfortunately, they will never see it.

Over the last decade or so, since my brilliant invention of the C.A.L.I.G.O device, I've found that obituaries have become my daily torture. At first, each name was a clear reminder that while the C.A.L.I.G.O device was a remarkable development and could prevent mass loss of life, it could not save everyone. Humanity's great purpose after all is to die.

Thomas Layton had another purpose though. His death was not just an end to life, but an artful stroke in the history books, one that would fuel the Great Northern Rebellion of 1978. Which would lead to the British Republic, the abolishment of the monarchy, a parliament reform, and the movement of the UK Capital to York, as per the Viking rule, a millennia ago. Thomas Layton's death at a riot on September 17th, 1978, would immortalise him as the people's champion, and would change the course of history for the rest of time. At least if time was left to run its proper course.

With my ground-breaking machine, that cast me into my godhood, I gave the ultimate political weapon over to the British government, and understandably after their collators received news of their future without their coveted power, they began to change things. Small things at first. Things such as which songs made it onto the radio. For instance, tracks by the Sex Pistols which would function as the anthem of that accursed rebellion were diminished and hidden from the public eye. Eddie and the Hot Rods who sang of independent thought and free will, daring to preach that everyone should do as they pleased, befell a series of events that could only be categorised as bad luck, and they too disappeared from the history books. Those who would show an interest despite this manipulation, were quickly quashed down and scorned by society. History was rewritten, black books recorded and issued to the correct agents. Whistle-blowers were silenced, and those who dared to speak out were ridiculed and pushed aside as malcontent wrong doers, who wanted to cause chaos and disrupt the status quo, which had worked so well for all these decades.

However, some disruptive types could not be manipulated by numbers, and could not be shuffled from the light. Types like Thomas Layton, who could rally the disadvantaged masses and could not be hidden from view. To deal with these stubborn few, those in charge turned to a more distasteful solution, the likes of which would not be approved by the Ethics Committee. Instead of dying in a political riot in six months' time, Thomas Layton suffered a heart attack in his sleep, passing away on February 28th, 1978. His death repurposed and his life reduced to a few lines of mediocrity.

I find that now I hate obituaries because there are names in them that are there far too early, because of me. I feel like Dr Frankenstein, as his monster rampages on unaware of the true nature of its damage, sometimes

I can almost hear its screams echoing back through time, as its purpose is corrupted. There is a storm raging outside, which I'm sure is nature itself screeching its accusations at me, as it is forced to bow to the will of foolish men obsessed with their power.

The rain pelts my expensive hide away, like a thousand angry fists thirsty for my blood. The thunder is a great booming command telling me to be afraid, warning me not to leave my lonely Mount Olympus of a great county house, with its grandiose furnishings, lest I be struck by its holy light that steals life from its vessels.

I raise my glass to Thomas Layton and all his unrealised potential, he deserved novels, statues, and chapters amidst history books, instead he got four lines in his local paper. The amber liquid in my crystal glass is worth a hundred times the paper in which Thomas Layton's life has been immortalised. I don't particularly savour the drink, personally I can't tell the difference between the expensive stuff and the supermarket own brand, but keeping the image up even in my reclusion, at least allows my mind the illusion it is all worth it. It probably isn't.

The fire in the hearth burns quietly, as though it too fears the water that batters my house; It Is natural to fear that which has the capability to destroy us. All those who worship are god-fearing, they fear their lack the true conviction in their beliefs, they fear the divine retribution that their idol holds over them. The Ministry of Time fear me. I know they do, even after my exile. They are right to, I muse to myself as I gaze at the collection of manilla folders on my great floor to ceiling shelves. I know their crimes. How they have stolen free will and abused my monster to their own ends. The universe screams outside my walls, its anger all-consuming and tortured. It is nothing compared to the tempest in me. I will destroy that which I have created, such is the right of any god when they have been displeased. I am most displeased.

E.A.

Chapter 5

Michael hissed gratefully as the handcuffs were released, he began stretching his fingers and examining the rotation of his wrist. He tried hard to remember whether such actions had hurt as much before he had woken up cuffed to a bed. There was a thin red line around his wrist now, that was hot to the touch. Finally, though, he was able to shuffle back, further up the bed, so he wasn't slumped half flat and half raised on it.

The duty doctor squinted at the head wound, as though it was a gateway into Michael's brain. Michael couldn't find it in him to object to the strange examination, he simply felt very tired now. He felt like he hadn't slept in decades, as though he had been dismantled and someone had forgot to put his battery back. Or maybe it was the exhaustion of a wasted fifteen years, hoping that today he would get to be the hero he had sacrificed his whole life to be, only to be told that he was the wrong one. The wrong brother. He should have known that it was Harry, evidently his ego had kept him from realising the truth, that Harry was the one destined for greatness not him. Mark should be here, Michael thought selfishly; he'd promised to be here when Michael finally realised just how unfair his life was, and what he was owed for living in his brothers shadow his whole life.

"It's not as bad as it could have been. Head wounds just bleed a lot, although you almost certainly have a concussion. Not much we can do for that this side of history though Mr Brown, 'cept give you a few aspirin. Even then, I don't know if I can even give them to you. I've got no idea what you're allergic to, or if where you're from painkillers have the same effect." Michael painfully raised his eyebrows at the man.
"I'm from 2005 not the year 5000, medicine can't have advanced that much in thirty years, I'm sure whatever you give me will be fine." He replied.

At least it explained why the doctor kept examining him like some new species; evidently, he thought that in the future, humans had evolved physiologically to never need pain relief. It was strange, but Michael could hear annoyance in his voice. He didn't remember the last time he'd been angry; it was actually quite soothing to the emptiness he could feel where his stomach should be. It was not a battery, but it stoked some long dead fire at the very centre of him, and he found he had some energy. Enough at least, to get away from the doctor in front of him.

"Alright." The man conceded, shaking his head as he pulled off the rubber gloves; he glided over to his trolley on his wheeled examination stool. "You must understand Mr Brown, this has never happened before. I have never had to treat anyone who is not from this correct time. Hell, nobody here has ever met anyone from the future apart from the Collators." He rummaged through several pill bottles and packets before he turned back to Michael and glided back across the floor. He offered a packet to Michael. It was Paracetamol. Michael resisted the urge to laugh.
"Yeah, this will be fine." He assured the doctor and made to get up.
"Where do you think you're going?" Michael paused as the emptiness reasserted itself in his gut. He had no where to go. He knew no one. His money was likely not valid, and there was nothing to his name.

There was however something he did know, if he had to stay in this hospital room any longer, he was going to scream.

"I need to figure out what I'm gonna do next." He replied.
"I want to monitor that concussion of yours, you're staying here." Michael sighed and reached for his things on the bedside table, he was leaving even if he had to fight his way out.

He paused as his fingers rested on his wallet, he had no valid money, but the doctor did, so perhaps he could solve two problems in one. He acted resigned and produced the fifty pounds he had from his wallet, watching as the doctor's eyes fell upon the money with something like hunger.
"Shame that my money is now completely useless, hardly like I can go and exchange it is it?" He asked aloud, trying to keep a jovial tone. In his peripheral, the doctor wetted his lips and stared at the cash with amazement.
"Well…" He stuttered out. "Perhaps I can help you with that? I could give you the equivalent?" He proposed eagerly. Michael hummed in thought. Sensing it was not enough, the doctor continued. "I could also of course let you go, as is your wish. You seem clear headed, and the pain killers should be sufficient." The man out of time smiled and nodded.
"Alright that sounds like a deal."

The doctor actually got up off of his stool to Michael's surprise, and jogged over to his desk, where he procured his wallet from the top drawer. "How much do

I owe you?" He asked breathlessly as he stopped back in front of Michael.

"A hundred." Michael replied clearly and confidently. He was pushing his luck certainly, but he hoped the doctor was eager enough for relics of the future that he would pay the price.

"Of course." He replied without a moment's consideration. Clearly Michael could have asked for more. The money exchanged hands.

"Where would you recommend, I could get a room for tonight?" He asked as he tucked the money into his wallet.

"YMCA probably." The short man responded absently, engrossed in his examination of the futuristic bills. Michael flashed a grateful smile that the man didn't see and quickly made for the exit.

Chapter 6

Michael had wandered far from the Ministry of Time, not knowing where he was going, only that he wanted to be as far away from that building as he could get on foot. London was surprisingly a lot worse than in his time. The city in 2005 was no great shining jewel, but it was certainly better than 1977. Bin bags were piled high on the streets, grime seemed inlaid in every brick he passed, and a grey smog blurred the sky. Cars that had looked old even in his childhood trundled past him, Ford

Cortina's, BMW 3 series', Daimlers' and for the more upmarket businessman, a Mercedes S-class. All with washed out colours, dirty whites, smeared silvers, dull reds, faded yellows and brown, so many brown cars. It was like walking in an old postcard.

People were buttoned up despite the hazy, late summer sun, and moved briskly as though they feared they would be accosted any moment, by someone demanding money and the clothes on their back. They all kept their gaze firmly on the ground in front of them, and as Michael examined those he passed, he was aware of the sea of grey and brown he moved between. Concrete skyscrapers absorbed the suns weak light that streamed through the gaps between buildings, large double deckers dominated the roads like red giants and black cabs raced through the streets like enormous black bugs.

Michael found himself on South Bank, where he was struck by the realisation that there was no London Eye overseeing the London skyline. Only more confirmation that he was not in his right time. His head throbbed, and he rested his forearms on the wall holding the Thames at bay. He was so far out of his time. There was no one here that knew him. He wouldn't even be born for another three years. His ID was completely invalid and would likely be put to better use as a joke card. No one even knew he was here. He had no birth certificate, no proof he even existed; because he didn't; he was an impossibility. He needed to go home.

Then something cold crept up his spine. Like the clawed hand of some horrible creature that has followed you for a while now, and just as you notice its presence, it pounces, desperate for its long-stalked meal. He could not go home. The C.A.L.I.G.O device that currently sat in the Ministry of Time was only ten years old, it could not travel to 2005, and the one from 2005 was now in 1967, its personal timeline was now out of sync with Michael's own. The most basic principle of the C.A.L.I.G.O device, was that both it and its occupants must be the same age in relation to their timeline. Michael was now undoubtedly, completely out of sync with the device that could get him home. He was stranded.

He would never be back in sync with the device from his time, he could travel in the device that was in the Ministry of Time now, but going back further was not going to help him. He wanted to go forward. He couldn't. Michael looked back up at the strange London before him, it would not be the London he knew for nearly thirty years, and if he wished to see his London, he would have to live through those thirty years and age with them. He would be fifty-two when he returned to his London. The emptiness was back with a vengeance, as the marionette strings that had carried him since he was ten, were cut from his body, seeking out a puppet worthy of their purpose. He collapsed to the miserable streets, that were too dirty and young to be the streets he knew. His back hit the wall, that had not yet weathered the storms he knew it would.

Michael was numb, as the too young city moved past him. Each second felt like an eternity, he wished each second was an eternity, so that he might blink, and his vision would be replaced by the city as it should be. The world felt unfinished and too sharp, like it had made spines to harm him, for it knew he was not where he belonged.

A small beep came from his pocket. Mechanically, he managed to coordinate himself enough to take a hold of his mobile. Like him, it was of another time. The Nokia flashed back its lack of signal, and Michael fell about into hysterical laughter. It racked his body like a deep ache beneath his ribs, that made him convulse and bend his body as close together as it could go, so as to protect the gaping hole at his centre. It wasn't until a while later, that he noticed his laughter had dissolved into tears streaming down his face that were not those of amusement, but pain. He heaved great sobs, that wracked his body. He was so utterly alone.

Eventually, he managed to force his body to stop, and carefully unclenched his hand from around his phone, that he had been squeezing painfully hard. Michael could feel the aches of the phantom misery throughout his body, and he forced his muscles to relax, stretching his legs out in front of him, across the width of the pavement. It was then, that the concussion made itself known to him properly, as it had failed to do before. His vision swam and his brain seemed to strain against his skull, like it had suddenly grown to twice its usual size.

Carefully, he reached into his other pocket and pulled out the paracetamol he had been given. Only then did he notice he did not have a drink on him, and at that moment he could not even comprehend the mechanics of standing to go and try and find a store, let alone the fact he was sure the ground was unfairly tilting beneath him.

Michael popped two pills into his hand and grimly forced them into his mouth, the bitter taste was immediately apparent, but he refused to throw up as he swallowed against his instincts. Eventually, when he could no longer feel them stuck in his throat, he breathed a sigh of relief. He closed his eyes against the nightmare that was his reality and waited for them to take effect.

After an indeterminable amount of time, the pressure on his head had returned to a dull ache and with regret, he began shakily making his way to his feet. The world had not stopped turning and he couldn't very well sit on the ground for the next thirty years. He turned back to the great river. From what little he could remember, there was a protocol in place for a man like him. The 'Timeless' protocol. It had never been used.

In the event that an agent fell out of sync with their correct device, they were to live out their life in the time they had joined, as though they had always belonged there. They were to dispose of all items from their time, so as to not disrupt the timeline with technology that had not yet been invented. Then the individual should report to whatever version of the Ministry of Time that existed, to receive a new identity and support.

Michael had no desire to face the Ministry again just yet, but he could follow at least some of it for the moment. He glanced down at the phone in his hand, in retrospect he should have traded it with the doctor for more money, but now he needed to get rid of it. He took another long look at the slow-moving water in front of him. He had once been told that time was like water, ever flowing, always moving forward. With every moment that passed he came closer to being home. Michael gripped the phone tightly, then launched it through the air. He watched as it spun and fell into the great mass of water, as it was carried downstream, a relic in time.

With that done, he set off again aimlessly wandering, he did not know this London, but he could come to learn it and perhaps eventually he would not notice a difference.

September 27ᵗʰ, 1980

Some days are noticeably important, even if nothing remarkable happens to you, as though the very air is charged with energy. On those days, I find myself to be more aware of the earth spinning on its axis, how our time is so small, barely a thread on the universe's great tapestry. On those days, you become aware I think, of the lucky few who do not blend into the deep throes of black that make up much of the great expanse, but instead are full of the silvery light of the stars, or the deep colour of a faraway nebula, or the majesty of a planet. Some though are even more special, they are incandescent with the universe's light and form the epicentre of a supernova.

It is my choices that have left my thread mangled and without any colour or life, a small anomaly in the beautiful eternity. I am grouped with those others who have a deficit of universal light, and my thread is a constituent of a black hole. It is lifeless and cancerous, as it steals the light for itself, but finds it is not a fitting receptacle, and so it destroys that which it covets. The universe's light will never fill me, I am not made of stardust like my fellow men, I am cursed to be this abomination I have always known myself to be. All my attempts to aid my fellow men, have resulted in nothing but destruction and misery. I am a black hole that dreams of being a star.

Today is not an important day. At least as far as the universe is concerned, it is undoubtedly still an important day for someone somewhere, babies are born, people die, people get married, but it is simply another day in which the world keeps turning, and twenty-four hours pass by, much as they did the day before. However, today the most important man in history was born. He was born seven pounds and six ounces to an ordinary couple in Greater Manchester they were Mr and Mrs Brown, and they named their new-born, Michael James Brown.

Michael was not outwardly special, and most would probably never consider him anyone of interest, but he was the thread that would make up the core of a supernova. His mind was a perfect mirror of the universe itself, and the universe would not be able to help itself but to fall madly in love with the boy, who shone back a perfect image of its own beauty. For that was Michael's gift, he was a still lake, unaffected by the winds of time, reflecting that which looked upon him.

Michael deserved a life full of joy, encompassed by the universe's love. Unfortunately, this is not the life he will receive because of me. I will ruin Michael Brown. I have already ruined him, and the worst part of it is that he thanked me for it. I grasped the starlight in his thread and took it for myself, only for it to slip through my fingers, as it was not made for me. I am not worthy of it.

There's a knock at the door. It is unusual for me to have visitors. I do not have friends. I am alone. I discard my crystal tumbler full of my expensive whiskey, it dances as though lit from within, as it refracts the light from the fire. It glitters like amber, like a small sun in my dark room. I straighten my shirt as is my habit, unsure why, as this is the same one I have worn for a week. The door is bolted shut and it takes me a moment to shift it from the stiff position, it is so used to shutting the world out. There's probably a metaphor there but I can't quite grasp it.

It is not who I expected to see. A sharply dressed man is stood in the drizzle, he is wearing various shades of grey. A lighter grey fedora adorns his head shielding his face, a deeper grey long trench coat protects his body. It is not done up. He does not expect to be stood here very long. He wears a medium grey suit beneath his jacket, and a white shirt. His tie is the same colour as his coat, or maybe it's not, it's difficult to tell in the little light.
"Elijah." He says, it is odd to hear another voice that is not my own.
"Christopher." I reply courteously.
"Can I come in?" He asks. I look down to the briefcase he clasps and nod my head, moving to the side to allow him entry.

He joins me in the only lived in room, where the fire is still quietly burning.
"Whiskey?" I ask, raising the decanter in question. He nods once, before taking the armchair opposite mine. I try very hard not to remember the last person who used to do that, and I hand him the twin tumbler to mine. I then pick my drink back up from the table where I had discarded it. Unlike my habit I do not lean back into my chair but rest forward with my forearms on my knees. Christopher is sat perfectly straight as he ever does. Not one motion of his is ever anything less than perfectly calculated and measured.
"I found some new ones for 1990, and there's also an early election report for June 7th, 2001, and how it was achieved." He procured the standard manilla folders from his briefcase, greedily I took them from him and scanned over their titles and dates. This was the only connection I had to the outside world.

"I also thought this was interesting." He said after a weighted moment. I looked up to see him offering what looked like an old school history textbook. Its pages were crumpled, and the corners curled and dog-eared. I took it from him with reverence and eased open the cover. It was dated 1983 as year of publishing. It was undoubtedly fascinating, but not something essential, I couldn't help but question why the Accountant had brought it for me.

"Why?" I managed with my rough voice of disuse or perhaps unquantifiable emotion.

"Happy Birthday." He told me simply.

"It is." I replied thinking about Michael. We sat in silence for a while, and I was uncharacteristically charitable in allowing him to examine me, uninhibited or regulated, as I read exerts from the textbook with its unexperienced events. It is strange to know that this is the true flow of time, and not this reality we have become so acclimatised to.

"I'll be the one bringing the files from now on." Christopher announced. I finally looked back up to him. What must I look like to him? Did he see me as a black hole? I assumed he must not, as if he did, he would not be sat across from me now. Christopher Stevens was a silvery shining moon in my eyes. He was a protector at heart, a man who was steadfast in his beliefs, one who maintained the light even in the darkest of hours; one of the few good men I have ever met. "I think it's for the best after what happened with Lizzie, don't you?" I had the good grace to look back down to the textbook at that.

Lizzie had brought the files for the last three years. It had been the only thing I had to look forward to. She was a pillar of the universe; so complex and full of life, like a whole planet inside one person. Being around her was like being around my C.A.L.I.G.O device once again, she was so full of untold knowledge, impossibility, and beauty it felt like she too, had been marked by my *creation. I was never alone when Lizzie was around. Then last month she had come over as usual, and like always she had tried to reach me, tried to ease my loneliness permanently. She held her hand out through the bars of my cage, offered me a life in which I would never have to be without her light again.*

The trouble with that is that I know myself. I know the selfishness at the heart of me, just as you do. If she had joined me, I would have swallowed her light in my desperation to be worthy of her, and instead, I would have condemned her to the same existence as me. To this hollow desperation full of the shadows of life. I couldn't do that. I have destroyed enough lives as it is. So, I let her see that true dark emptiness that resides where my light should be, and finally her survival instinct kicked in and she ran away from my cage.

"Yes, it's probably for the best." I replied. Christopher gave a short nod and downed the remaining amber liquid in his glass with decisive movements, so unlike my hesitant posturing. With that, he stood and made his way to the door. I followed him through, and watched with intrigue as he donned his hat and coat. He opened the door, and the rhythmic pitter patter of rain filled the vacuum of the hall.
"Lizzie deserves better than you." He said quietly. Ah, so the moon was shielding the planet from its own destruction.

"She does." I confessed. He nodded again and strode back out into the night.

I returned to my room, where the fire had finally dimmed. I picked up my glass once again toasting Michael James Brown. Today was not an important day.

E. Ainsley

Chapter 7

By Michael's increasingly rough estimation he had been walking aimlessly for nearly two hours. He forced his legs to stop as he exited Hyde Park. Michael had tried to reassure himself by visiting the landmarks he knew well from his London, but if anything, it was simply making his discomfort worse. Big Ben, Buckingham Palace, Westminster Bridge, Kensington Palace they were just not quite right.

Michael took in his surroundings as he entered Notting Hill Gate, it looked far from the affluent, busy thoroughfare it was in 2005. Newspapers and rubbish littered the pavement like leaves in autumn. It looked as though London were preparing for a harsh winter and so had shaken its branches, abandoning that which it could not sustain or look after. Shops were shut and boarded up, with old flyers blowing in the wind promising a sale. It was a shell of what it should be.

The London of 1977 was very different to the London of 2005. In Michael's time the city was a bustling hub of modern technology, people talking on small phones or into Bluetooth headsets. The roads were swarmed with shiny Ford Fiesta's, Ford Galaxy people carriers together with the upmarket Mercedes and BMW's that were all smooth curves, boisterous colours that sat in gridlock. The 2000's were all bright displays of humanity's technological advancements, its edges were soft, sleek, and polished. It was welcoming.

Michael waded through the sea of rubbish and old print, as he gazed around at the ghost town that should have brought him comfort. He realised only then that he knew very little about 1970s Britain. This was when a historian would come in useful, because the only thing that was clear to him was that 1977 was not a good year. It was cold, sharp, and unwelcoming, not that there was an idyllic time Michael had in mind, but he rather thought he would have been hard pressed to find a time so clearly miserable. The architecture was harsh as it consisted primarily of varying shades of grey concrete; peeling paint and posters adorned the walls and lamp posts. Roads and pavements seemed to be crumbling to pieces beneath the weight of the city and cracks covered every surface.

Across the road, Michael finally caught his first sign of life since he had left Westminster; a man leant against the grime covered brickwork. He had long hair that reached his elbows, and wore brown flared trousers, an off-white baggy shirt, and a faded denim jacket. His eyes were covered by large dark sunglasses, that watched his hands as he tapped out a rhythm on his thighs. Next to him, on a grey-washed wall the words 'Power to the People, Right On' were spraypainted.

Michael found himself frozen in place as the man looked up at him. It was the first time he had actually been acknowledged by someone from this time that wasn't from the Ministry. Until that moment Michael had been entertaining some desperate hope that perhaps no one could see him. He shivered in the small breeze as he held eye contact with the strange man from behind his dark shades. It was a stark contrast from the city centre, where people had watched the pavement and refused to acknowledge anyone around them. His concentration was broken, as he became aware of a sound other than far-away cars, crinkling paper and the whistling breeze.

There was music in the air. Michael whipped his head around searching for the source of the brilliant clashing sound of excitement in this drab city. A little way up on the left, there was one small shop that was not covered in sale stickers or closing down notices. Instead, there were great posters full of colour and record cover art in the window. The store front was painted a bright red and shining gold lettering proclaimed the oasis as the 'Virgin Record Store'.

Michael pushed inside the shop, eager for this sign of life, enjoyment, and difference from the miserable conformity of grey and brown outside. Once he stepped through the door it was like rising above water, and finally the muffled sound of life became clear. He hadn't even realised how muted the world had felt until this very moment. Over loudspeakers, came what he struggled to categorise as music as he had ever known it.

The defiant, angry vocals matched the hollow monster that had recently made its home in Michael. It was the first comfort he had found since arriving here, that maybe someone else felt like he did, that he was not as alone as he had thought.[1]

The lyrics expressed every thought, fear and sentiment Michael had forbidden himself to consider throughout his teenage years. The years he had lost as a result of the black book that sat even now in his back pocket. These are the words he should have been listening to his whole life. Not the treacherous, deceiving commands gifted to him as a child. Those words that had kept him placated, quiet and obedient

---

[1] God Save the Queen – The Sex Pistols

had led him to nothing but misery. This was the truth right here. There was no future for him, at least not one worth having. This nothing future he was now living in the past because of his blind obedience to a book given to him by a man who had hoped to tell him how to live his life. He had fallen for it with its promises of riches and reverence, but maybe if he had heard these words instead, he might not have had the future he was 'supposed' to have but maybe he would have been happier.

He looked around at the store that was full of bright colours which filled every inch of space. Singles adorned spinning racks that towered up to six feet high, along the walls, shelves proudly displayed mint condition famous records and the currently charting albums. Around the room cardboard boxes contained hundreds of vinyl albums with handwritten sticky labels displaying the genre or artist. It was a sanctum of life amidst this decaying society Michael found himself in.

He made his way up to the counter, where the cashier stood reviewing the back of an album. She looked different. A good different, as she was covered in vibrance. Her hair was streaked with several shades of pink and purple, which clashed with her bright, ugly green, baggy tank top, tattoos ran up her arms and bright shiny silver piercings shone from her ears. She was strikingly different.

"Excuse me!" He had to raise his voice over the music. She looked up with a bored expression as she regarded his grey clothing and dull features, before flicking up to his forehead where the large plaster disrupted the unimaginative impression that Michael gave off.
"What." She said bluntly.
"This track, what's it called?" He asked undeterred. Her brow furrowed for a moment, as though she didn't understand his question. "I haven't heard it on the radio." He elaborated, as though trying to assure her of his existence in this time. Not that she would ever have guessed he was from the future, because that was, for most people, completely preposterous.

"You won't have done, but surely you read the papers or watch the telly?" She said with an amused smile as though she was unsure whether he was joking.
"Not really, I'm not that up to date with current events." He said smiling back at her.
"You must live under a rock then." She shook her head in disbelief. "It's called 'God Save the Queen' by the Sex Pistols, its about anarchy and rebellion against the bastards that have fucked up our country." She replied, her tone uncompromising, reaching for the single by her record player. It was a deep blue, with a crude picture of the Queen edited with safety pins, the proud title and band name covered her eyes and mouth written in ransom note format. It was certainly a statement.

"It's brilliant." He said, astonished and enraptured. There was nothing like this in 2005. No one talked of these things. Michael hadn't allowed himself to so much as think these thoughts let alone express them. He had been so afraid of the conclusions he might have come to. That those conclusions would not match with those of his superiors, or with the ending the black book had given him. Perhaps it was this kind of prevention of free thought that had led to the corruption at the heart of the Ministry, with no one left to offer a differing opinion the politicians had been able to do whatever they liked.

She seemed surprised at his exclamation but smiled conspiratorially and leaned across the counter. "Did you know it was supposed to be number one, but they changed it at the last minute and refused to air it?" She asked excitedly as though discussing some sort of scandalous gossip.
"Really?" He asked astonished.
"They couldn't have the 'filth and the fury' on air." She said snidely and moved to the record player to put a new track on.
"How much damage could one track do?" Michael asked, confused.

"It's not about the music, it's about the people." She replied matter of factly. Michael looked up from the single to her. That was certainly true. Most things in life came down to people rather than things themselves Michael was coming to learn. Surely if enough people where he was from could listen to this, and allow themselves to question that which they were told were already foregone conclusions, the Ministry would not have gotten away with all that it had?

"Do you believe in a rebellion?" He asked seriously. Matching her tone.
"I believe you should have the free will to do what you want, and no one should be able to tell you otherwise." She replied evasively but no less honest.
"And what if what you want to do, is what everyone else is telling you to do." Michael philosophised, thinking of Ainsley and his life which still hung in the balance. It was not the inventor's fault that the Ministry had corrupted C.A.L.I.G.O's purpose.
"Then at least you did it by your own choice, and not just because they forced you to."

Michael breathed a shaky sigh of relief at her words as his traitorous hands itched to hold his black book.
"Thank you." He said, with the weight of a man who had just been told every thought and doubt of his was okay and had been understood in just a few words. She looked at him worriedly for a moment, her eyes rested on his forehead for a moment before returning eye contact.
"You want the record?" She asked moving away from ideology.

"Ummm, can you put it on hold for me?" He asked. He'd be back to get it, there was just some things he had to do first.

"'Course I can. What's your name?"

"Michael Brown." She scribbled it on a sticker which she then stuck on the record.

"Alright Mike, I'll see you around." He nodded, bewildered at the nickname, and left the shop full of life and its answers.

This time he noticed as his mind was submerged beneath the dim, murky shadow of 1970s London. The man with long hair was gone, but the writing was not. He looked further up the street where he had come from and turned in the direction he had yet to venture. He began his mindless wandering once again.

As he left Notting Hill Gate, Michael was pleasantly encompassed by people once again, but unlike the sea of grey and brown overcoats that streamed through Westminster, here colour was fighting back against the bleak, industrial feel of the city. Women wore luscious fur coats, wax anoraks, or long patterned wool jackets, paired with varying lengths of chequered skirts or flared jeans for the younger women. There were no prominent labels or brands like most people wore in the 2000s. The men wore two-piece suits in varying conservative colours but unlike the businessmen of the city centre they held their heads high and met the gaze of their fellows with a recognising smile. Some more tradesman types dressed in double denim or flared jeans, a simple t-shirt, and a biker style jacket. The colours did not pop with artificial strength that clashed with others but instead coalesced into a beautiful kaleidoscope of life.

The shops were each specialised, butchers, greengrocers, pharmacies, budget homeware stores, and grandiose department chains. It was very different to those convenience supermarkets and the branded outlets of the future Michael was familiar with. There was a greater sense of community amongst the sellers and their loyal customers despite the unfinished air about the buildings. Life here felt raw, like it was missing the perfect plastic film Michael was used to looking through.

Michael thought on his discussion with the record seller; he didn't want to do what the book told him to, not after finding out it was not his to follow in the first place. Not when it was the reason, he had lost all sense of freedom. However, Elijah Ainsley was still in danger, and his brother was not going to save him. There was no future awaiting him, no great purpose left to fulfil, unless he made it so. He was no longer a slave to the contents of the black book, but he was rather out of practice with making decisions, there was nothing telling him specifically, to save the man, but if he wasn't saved, then the whole of time could collapse. Michael could wash his hands of the whole thing and move on in 1977, or he could follow through on what he had spent his whole life preparing for and return here anyway, with the knowledge that he was better man. Michael supposed it all came down to one question. Did the great Professor Elijah Ainsley deserve his help?

He meandered with the crowd down the street; it would be a lot easier if he had the Professors' address or phone number. Though from what he remembered from all his extensive research of the man, he was currently guest lecturing around the country this year and could be at any university anywhere in England. Well, that wasn't strictly true, in October, Professor Ainsley would do his final lecture and become a recluse for no known reason. His final lecture had been at Imperial College London, where he had guest lectured for his final two weeks from the 23rd of September. So, Ainsley could theoretically be in London right now at the university, but Michael had no idea what the exact date was.

Further ahead of him was a newspaper stand and Michael pushed his way quickly through the throng of people. The man looked up at him in surprise as Michael produced a twenty-pound bill.
"They're 6p mate, I haven't got change for that."
"I haven't got anything else."
"Then it'll cost you eleven pounds fifty-four cos I haven't got that much change."
"Yeah fine." Michael replied too eager to get his hands on the paper.

"Must be alright up North." The man muttered as he pocketed the note. They swapped over and Michael stuffed the change in his pocket. The date was the 30th of September, a Friday. Michael rifled through the paper and finally came across Professor Ainsley's face. The paper congratulated him on a successful week of lectures at the Imperial College University, and his success on inspiring the young minds of the next generation of physicists.

"Thanks!" Michael called to the man as he set off in search of a bus stop.

November 6th, 1982

It is times like these I fear Orwell was right. He almost had the timeline right as well considering todays date. The Ministry of Time is certainly my Big Brother, I no longer think they are afraid of me. No, I have this terrible feeling they have spent the last fifteen years lulling me into a false sense of security, allowing my arrogance to do the work for them. Or maybe my reclusion has been my mistake, perhaps they believe I have hidden away from the world to protect myself, rather than to protect the world from me.

My lawyer sits in the armchair across from me, I am having my will drawn up, as I'm unsure whether I shall be sitting in this chair at the end of the week. I have no doubt that should I meet my untimely end before the week is out, that the Ministry of Time will challenge the will I make tonight. After all, it is not beyond the realm of possibility that I have gone completely round the bend, but I think knowing the truth about this world is more than reason enough to be a little insane. However, I have taken every precaution to ensure that does not happen, my estate and all assets monetary or otherwise have been left to Christopher Stevens, all scripts and novels within my possession are left to Alison Thomas, my personal diary and effects including a certain black book are left to Elizabeth Jones. It is also my wish that my body be donated to science, in the hope that it will provide more use to alleviating our human condition than my mind has.

The greying law man asks me if I'm sure about these decisions, he reminds me gently that I do not have friends or family, and he carefully asks if I'm being taken advantage of. It's almost funny. I reassure him that there's no one influencing my decisions, after all my paranoia is hardly its own entity. Or maybe it is?

Eventually I satisfy his concerns and usher him from my cave. I turn the rarely used electric lights off and the room is plunged into the smoky darkness I have come to appreciate. A pale, blue, light streams through my window, the starlight falls just short of my chair. By memory I pick up my packet of 'light' cigarettes, and my suitably expensive lighter; I took up smoking to give myself a hobby, since drinking my single malt was no longer as enjoyable as I'd thought. The idea of 'light' cigarettes still makes me chuckle.

On the side table lies the reason for the hasty meeting with my lawyer. I had received a letter this morning from my former employer, requesting a meeting in five days' time. It is suitably vague on the details of what the meeting is about, and after reading some highly classified files that have been smuggled to me, I have no illusions about the lengths the Ministry are willing to go to. I take a long drag of my cigarette, and ease back in my chair that now holds a perfect imprint of me. It is good to know that if nothing else, this chair shall remember me, if only the shape of my less flattering side.

Should they attempt to eliminate me in the coming days, I will of course welcome death with open arms. After all, I can hardly blame them for doing what I have often considered. I am a blight on this earth, and it is only human nature to destroy that which may hinder our continued existence. There is only one reason I have not taken my own life, and that reason is that someone must watch the Ministry, someone has to be aware of what has been changed, someone must carry that burden of knowledge. This burden has been mine to carry since I created my monster, it is my comeuppance for my sins, and I will not shy from the punishment that has been designed for me. I will not add coward to my list of crimes.

I take peace in the clear night and the starshine that provides the little light in my room, perhaps I still have time.

Elijah Ainsley

Chapter 8

Michael thanked the driver as he stepped off the bus, his incredibly expensive newspaper clasped in his hands. He had taken the chance to read it on the journey, which had left him feeling a little shakier about his chances of living well in 1977. There had been intermittent strikes throughout England this year, with the papers convinced it was only going to get worse in the coming years. That at least explained the rubbish bags that lined the streets like new cornerstones. The Government seemed to be making no progress in resolving pay disputes and society appeared to be on the brink of breaking beneath the weight of its problems. Evidently, he'd picked the wrong year to become 'Timeless'.

He gazed up at the Blackett Laboratory; he had been here once before in 1999 to see a lecture by Ainsley himself, and even now he could remember every word the man had spoken, how he had held the room in the palm of his hand. Michael couldn't deny he was intrigued as to what the man was like as a young pioneer, before his reclusion from society. Whether Ainsley would be as captivating, as commanding, or as cryptic as he had been in Michael's memory.

The building was as unimpressive as ever, it was clad in a sickly shade of light green, that too was coated in the horrible grime London seemed to be painted with. It was rather typical of the time he was in now and didn't look out of place amidst the built for purpose style architecture that surrounded it. The building was entirely symmetrical, and your gaze almost passed over it for its lack of impressive features. For what Michael was coming to understand as a time period full of potential for change, rebellion and non-conformity, their imagination was severely lacking. Buildings consisted of hulking concrete, sometimes overlaid with corrugated metal and others left bare as unimaginative and undefined masses.

The bus drove past him, disrupting him from his reverie and Michael crossed over to the mundane university. Thankfully he was young enough that he could still pass for a university student, so no one stopped him as he entered the building and moved through the cold corridors, following the posted signs to Ainsley's lecture hall. Michael soon came across a mass of people that took up the whole width of the corridor. He pressed himself to the wall to avoid being swept away amongst the mass of excited physics students, who Michael was willing to bet had just attended the most interesting lecture of their whole life. Eventually the large stampede was reduced to a trickle of students and Michael could breathe again as he continued on to find the Professor.

Finally, he arrived at the door and Michael took a deep steadying breath, he knew what just being in the same room as Elijah Ainsley felt like. He couldn't yet imagine what having all that rapt, all-seeing attention fixed on him would be like, especially without the safety of a crowd to hide behind. After calming himself as much as possible, he pressed his hand on the door and entered the room.

It looked much the same as it had 1999, the walls were high reaching slabs of varnished wood, which had also been used to build the rows of benches. A deep teal green had been used to cover the backs of the concave benches, the seats were segregated by small planks of wood, and the flip down cushions were all upright, awaiting the next influx of students. There was a large blackboard behind the great wooden desk at the far end of the lecture hall, that stretched the width of the room, it had been painted with chalk in the language of the universe. The artist stood with his back to Michael, admiring his art.

"I'm sorry the lecture's over, if you've missed it, I'm here all next week." Came the practiced, enticing voice of Professor Elijah Ainsley the Godfather of Time Travel.
"I-I'm not here for the lecture." Michael stuttered out. Ainsley turned to look up the lecture hall, where Michael stood staring down at him. Ainsley was a man of a similar height and build to Michael, with messy dark curls, that framed his still quite boyish looks for a man in his thirties. He had a sharp nose, and clear pale blue eyes that seemed alight from within. His skin was slightly tanned, contrasting his white shirt and complimenting the deep maroon three piece of suit, which he wore like a man who had been raised in the upper folds of society. He raised his amber, round framed glasses off his face and placed them in his hair.
"Then what are you here for?" Elijah watched him with what could only be characterised as intrigue.
"To figure out if your life is worth saving."

Ainsley tilted his head, a bemused smiled appearing on his face.
"Are you here to kill me?" He asked, his tone bordering on uninterested, and Michael had to wonder whether the Professor had much experience with people trying to kill him.
"No, but there is a man who has travelled to 1967 to do so." He explained in a disconcerted tone.
"Ah I see. So, what exactly would make me worthy of your help Agent?" Still Ainsley talked as though this was

simply an interesting thought experiment, or some small anomaly in his life that Michael had brought to his attention.

The question rather stumped Michael, who had never had to preside over what qualities and achievements would make one worthy of the life they had already lived. As if sensing Michael's inner struggle, he smiled. "While you mull that over, perhaps you could join me down here, so I don't have to crane my neck looking up to you." Ainsley gestured for him to walk down the stairs, as he moved to behind the desk and began shuffling papers. Michael found his head throbbing more painfully now than it had been earlier, and he wasn't sure if it was due to the painkillers wearing off, or Ainsley's strange behaviour.

As he descended, the Professor pulled out a bottle of Bell's Whiskey, which he set on his desk along with two short glasses. He then moved to the corner of the room, where a spare chair had been resting and moved it to the opposite side of the desk. He caught sight of the bewildered look on Michael's face as he got closer and he smiled genuinely at him and gestured for him to take the new chair as he collapsed on his own.

Michael didn't understand. This was not going how he thought it would. There was no endless questioning, no shouting, no demands, or pleas. Instead, the man sat there with that damnable calm radiating from him, and

Michael's head hurt something fierce. He felt that new anger brimming, how it filled up the emptiness and demanded action, demanded a change, control. How do you start the conversation in which you accuse the man in front of you of ruining your whole life? How do you tell him that he's the reason you never got to make a choice or decide your own fate? How his ridiculous invention and all the stupid responsibility that comes with it, has ruled your life since you were ten years old? How do you tell him that the only reason you are trapped thirty years in the past, before you are even born, is because you were told you had to save his life? How do you then explain that you're actually the wrong man?

Chapter 9

Michael reached into his back pocket and pulled out the black book, which he threw to the desk. Ainsley blinked in almost astonishment, as though Michael was not playing to the script. He reached carefully for the small pocketbook. With reverence, he began to read it, each page, each instruction, Michael's whole life, in a small book. It was a quick read. The Professor closed it and laid it delicately on the desk. He said nothing, but uncorked his bottle and poured a large measure in both glasses. "Have a drink."

"Why?" Michael asked croakily, the turbulent emotions that had followed him all day had seemed to settle on his throat as he stood in front of the man that was the cause of them.

"Does the book tell you to have a drink?" Ainsley looked to have aged before his eyes, as he demanded the answer.

"No."

"Then drink." Michael approached the desk. He sat gratefully in the chair, before reaching for the glass and tipping back a good amount. It burned as it ran down his throat, though he was grateful for it as it slackened the chokehold of emotion.

"What's your name?" The Professor asked his saviour, all humour and disinterest gone from his voice.

"Michael Brown." Ainsley nodded, taking it in like he was committing it memory.

"You're from 2005?" He asked. Michael confirmed with a shake of his head.

"How old are you?"

"Twenty-four."

"Fourteen years…" He hissed under his breath. "You gave up your whole life for me? For this horrific book?" Michael was shocked at the obvious anger in Ainsley's sharp blue eyes. He had heard others speak of the Professor's legendary temper, how he was like a raging fire that scorched those around him. Now though, as he sat in the presence of Ainsley's anger, it felt more like a vast ocean in a storm. It was an all-enveloping, suffocating anger, that came in relentless waves.

Michael felt his own rising to meet it. Ainsley had no right to be angry, he had not lived Michael's life, and was only set to reap the rewards of Michael's sacrifice. "Of course! I was told I would save the great Professor Ainsley, inventor of Time Travel and save the whole damn universe, by keeping time flowing as it should! You don't get to judge my life, or how I've lived it, not when it's because of your damn device that this can even happen in the first place!"

Ainsley opened his mouth as if to interrupt, but Michael spoke louder, drowning out any complaint, meeting Ainsley's tempestuous ocean with the tsunami of unvoiced thoughts that had built in his subconscious mind for nearly fifteen years. He was relentless, as every spiteful and despairing thought he had experienced over the last few hours left his mouth. "I'm not going to be born for another three years! I'm also trapped here in this godawful decade because I got it wrong!" He struggled to prevent his voice from cracking under the weight of emotion that a day ago he was unaware humans were capable of experiencing. It strangled him, like a phantom weight against his throat that made his vision blurry as he tried to breathe. His body forced out the words that it could no longer contain, for they were poisoning him from inside his mind. "I'm not supposed to be here! It was supposed to be my brother." Michael heaved a deep breath as he finished his outburst, forcing oxygen down his throat, and swallowing heavily against the pain he could feel rising, like bile. He was triumphant, as the sea of rage in Ainsley's eyes calmed, shocked still by Michael's pain.

It took Ainsley a few minutes to find his voice. "I'm sorry. You're right of course." Ainsley leaned back in his chair, taking what seemed to be a steadying sip of his own drink. He gave Michael a moment to compose himself before continuing in a softer voice. "I just can't help but feel responsible. This book," He picked the black book up and waved it beside his head, Michael was startled by the similarity of the professor's image to that of Elizabeth Jones' interrogation that morning. "Is only proof that my device, and the Ministry of Time have long since lost any basis in ethics. And your presence here, only tells me that my mistake in trusting in them is so *catastrophic*, that someone would destroy the flow of time, to remove me, and my poor judgement." Michael was surprised by the venom and despair in the Professor's quiet voice, and suddenly his anger felt wrong in the face of a man so clearly full of self-loathing, he did not need Michael's own derision on top of that. They sat in silence for another moment, as their emotions lay heavy in the air.

"What did you mean that your brother is supposed to be here?" Ainsley asked, trying to move away from the more painful topics. Michael looked down at the glinting amber liquid, Ainsley's first peace offering. A choice.

"My brother Harry. He's an Executor in 2005, he was supposed to get the black book not me." Michael explained tiredly, taking another smaller sip of the expensive liquor. Ainsley frowned.

"When were you given the book exactly?" He asked.

"On my tenth birthday."

"Is Harry your twin?"

"No?" Michael replied confused.

"Then I doubt that someone would hand the book they thought would prevent the collapse of reality, to the wrong boy on his birthday." With that sentence alone, Michael felt something that had been torn begin to piece together again. Not entirely, the scar and feelings that had come with it would never fade, but perhaps it would not become this gaping wound he carried around like a lost limb. Ainsley flashed him a small smile as though he understood the intense relief Michael had just experienced.

"So, I suppose that leaves the most obvious question, what are you doing here in 1977 if I'm going to die ten years ago?" Ainsley asked taking another sip of whiskey, an inkling of his sharp amusement returning to the cadence of his voice.

"I wasn't piloting the 2005 C.A.L.I.G.O device, your assassin was, he threw me out." Michael replied haltingly, wincing at the memory of his failure.

"And that's when you got your concussion?" Ainsley said with a smile, seemingly unconcerned with Michael's pitiful defeat. His blue eyes flicked to Michael's forehead, and he motioned to the plaster with a sympathetic grin.

"Yeah." Michael reached up and touched the cotton edge, it seemed if he was waiting for Ainsley to be angry with him, he was to be sorely disappointed and he felt a bashful smile creep onto his face. Ainsley had proved from the beginning that he was not at all what Michael had been expecting and inexplicably he did not seem to blame Michael for his errors.

"But surely that means you're now out of sync with the device that could take you home?" Ainsley asked with what looked like pained hesitance, like he was hoping that he wasn't the one breaking this news to him.

"Yes, I'm stuck in 1977." Michael confirmed keeping everything neutral, his smile dropping from his features. He refused to allow that new fierce anger to rear its head. He had just reprimanded himself for his reactions to Ainsley's questions and Ainsley had proved himself understanding and careful with the universal calamity that was now Michael Brown's existence.

"And how are you taking that?" Ainsley probed further with empathetic reluctance. Michael laughed, it was not a sound he had ever heard himself make, it was a laugh full of pain and bitterness, neither of which were emotions he had ever experienced before today.

"Well." He said pointedly, biting down hard on his lip to keep to politeness. Ainsley gave a grim smile.

The Professor drummed his fingers a few times on his desk, seemingly considering something. "There isn't much I like about 1977 either, but I'll tell you what the music isn't bad." With that the Professor stood and moved to the small record player against the wall. Next to it was a black and silver record case which he clicked open. Michael watched as he carefully flicked through his collection, all of which were encased in plastic wallets, before taking one record out. Michael was a little sceptical, but after the record shop that morning he was more than well acquainted with the strange power music had to make him feel totally and completely understood, and right now he was desperate for just about anything that would make his life a little more bearable.

The vinyl began to spin, and the speaker crackled to life under the needle. Ainsley retook his seat opposite Michael; it was not like the hard sound of the Sex Pistols that he had heard in the record store but was again not like the hits of the 2000s. He closed his eyes and focused on the lyrics.[2]

Michael found himself grinning again and he opened his eyes to see Ainsley smiling back and tapping his desk

---

[2] Do Anything You Wanna Do – Eddie and the Hot Rods

in an impromptu drum solo. The feeling of being understood returned. It was like finally the universe and his mind were in equilibrium and the unpleasant feeling of being out of place that had plagued him since his arrival in 1977 fizzled away like the ache of a departed pain.

"I think, Professor Ainsley, that maybe 1977 isn't as bad as I feared it might be." Michael told the inventor in front of him, a true smile on his face for the first time in almost fifteen years. The Professor shook his head with amusement at the statement.
"I think Michael, that we have been far too intimately acquainted with each other's lives to be using such formal address, don't you?" Michael ducked his head in acceptance.
"I think so, Elijah."

January 19th, 1985

It is strange letting go of your creation, whether it be by your own volition, or you are forcibly separated from it. I imagine what I am feeling now is much like a parent watching their child become independent. The Ministry is too old now to suffer my overbearing oversight, and despite knowing they took very little of my warnings or censures to heart, there is nothing I can do to stop them. They are entity unto themselves now and they have long since operated outside of the British Government. The Ethics Committee is more a piece of flimsy warning tape around the cage of some dark, ravenous creature.

I have had very little involvement in the Ministry over the last few years its true, but today it became official. I knew it was coming after my refusal three years ago to build them another C.A.L.I.G.O device, that day I had struggled not to laugh at them. There was no future in which I would ever give them another weapon, not after I had seen their misuse of my first gift. Today I was called in and asked to sign more paperwork and contracts than I had ever seen. Most of which revolved around the glorious piece of legislation that is the Official Secrets Act, and enough Non-Disclosure Agreements that I fear I may not speak of anything that I did over the last nearly twenty years.

My record player circles lazily in the corner of my room, it blares music from a different lifetime. It is an ancient echo of what could have been, what should have been if I had not unleashed my monster unto this world. The long-faded voices call out for a rebellion, for their freedom to choose to be returned to them. This loss of free will shall be my legacy to this diseased world.

This is the only conclusion that I can draw from my plethora of failures and misjudgements, this world is diseased by our presence. Our selfishness and power-hungry ways lead us only into destruction, and the universe would be better off without us and our poisonous ambition. We are built with this straining need to be more than we are, to become gods, but we are undeserving of such dreams.

Something must be done about the Ministry of Time, someone must set right my mistakes and return humanity to its prideful mediocrity, rather than this god like imitation that they are unworthy of. I have this terrible feeling that this someone must be me; that the universe is taking its revenge upon the both of us. I must take on my terrible godhood that I have pandered after, to set right my foolish mistakes.

Though if this is how the universe sees fit to punish me, who am I to complain? I have played by the rules for my whole existence, but I think it is time the Ministry plays by mine and suffer for their transgressions against their God.

Professor E. Ainsley

Chapter 10

Michael felt his whole-body jump when the lecture hall doors slammed open. It was strange, but until that moment he had forgotten anyone else existed except him and Elijah. "Professor Ainsley!" Came a man's voice.

Michael whipped around, his body tensing with fear that somehow the assassin had changed his mind and had come to 1977 to carry out his mission. Instead, a different kind of terror filled him as he set eyes on A Division. They were a well-practiced unit, with Jones and Stevens side by side, leading their Chameleon and Historian into the room.

Out of the corner of his eye, Michael saw Elijah's face harden into an expression he hadn't yet seen on the Professor's face, it was similar to the anger he had witnessed earlier, and still not quite the same. A cool detachment had taken a hold of the Professor's usually expressive face and he leant back in his chair putting his feet up on the corner of his desk, regarding their advancement with the distant gaze of a scientist observing ants, in his glacier blue eyes.

Michael stood up as they finally finished their descent of the stairs, angling his body so that their view of Elijah was obscured. Until he knew why they were here, Michael was not of a mind to let them anywhere near the Professor, who clearly was not pleased by their presence. He got his first look at the remaining members of the 1977 A Division. Alison Thomas, their Chameleon, had black hair that was half tied back, and half spooling over her shoulders, her eyes were filled with kindness and sat inlaid in her face like gemstones. A black cardigan was draped over her white blouse, and she wore brown jeans held up with a black leather belt.

Charlie Morris was far less fashion forward and wore a simple black band t-shirt that Michael had never heard of and black jeans to match. His brown hair was limp and fell into his eyes behind thickly framed glasses. Morris presented Michael with his first real similarity between 1977 and 2005 and it was not a comforting similarity, he was a miserable husk-like image as all Historians were, haunted by their knowledge.

"What do you want?" Ainsley asked, his voice cool and devoid of any of its previous excitement or emotion. Michael regretted that he could no longer see Elijah's face but from the looks on A Division's faces he was hardly a welcoming sight. Morris even managed to scowl deeper as he fixed his despondent gaze on the Professor.
"The Ministry has just been shut down by the Ethics Committee." Stevens informed them, his face a mask of indifference, as was the standard expression for an Accountant.
"Yes, I'm not surprised, we took a vote last night on the proposed Phoenix mission, and it has not had the go-ahead. This is protocol if the Ministry tries to go against the ruling of the Committee." Elijah nodded his head in the direction of Charles Morris. "I'm surprised your historian didn't tell you that." Morris glared darkly at the Professor with something frighteningly similar to hatred flashing in his eyes. Elijah only maintained his outward disinterest as he sipped his whiskey,

unconcerned with the danger lining the Historian like a second shadow.

"You have to override the decision." Jones announced, and with that level of command and authority in her tone, Michael thought that God himself would have struggled to deny her. In response Ainsley's blue-grey eyes glittered in what looked like cold malice. The roiling ocean that had been frozen by their arrival, thawed in obvious cruelty and outrage at having been instructed to do anything.
"I will do no such thing. Just because you are mildly important to the Ministry does not make you important to me." He smirked in the face of Jones' own annoyance. The Executor seemingly did not possess her Accountant's ability to remain emotionless in the face of the Professor, as displeasure tainted her features. "I do not owe you anything and I will certainly not help you subvert your overseers, not when they have finally stood by their morals."

Their Chameleon, Alison Thomas rolled her eyes at the defiant staring contest between Jones and Ainsley, the air between them looked to be charged with unfriendly energy. It was clear to Michael that there was some history between the two of them. "We're not asking you to overturn the ruling on the Phoenix mission. We just need the C.A.L.I.G.O device running so we can go back to 1967 and save your life." Alison interjected. Michael raised his eyebrows at that; he had not expected A

Division to continue with the mission after it had gone wrong.

"And how do I know you're telling the truth?" Ainsley countered, ignoring Jones, and focusing on Thomas now. "How do I know you are not the assassins? I won't be a willing participant in my own murder." He said snidely.

"They're not though." Michael put in quietly, desperate to reduce the tension. Elijah looked up to him and lowered his feet from the desk.

"Of course, they're not, they're nowhere near intelligent or suicidal enough to try and murder me." Jones strode forward and elbowed Michael away from the desk, which she then slammed her hands down on. Elijah smiled, but kept his eyes fixed on Michael as if they were still the only two in the room.

"Listen Ainsley, we know you don't like us, and we don't like you, but right now we have a common interest, ensuring reality doesn't fall apart around us. If you can't get over your own ego and help us, then all that will be on your head." Lazily, Ainsley turned his gaze to Jones, Michael could feel the control that he had over the five of them, as their focus did not waver from the inventor.

"My ego?" He said, quietly, that bland smile still on his face, as he held Jones' glare. "It was not my ego that had the audacity to tell a man, who had just sacrificed everything, that he was the wrong boy. You turned away his help because some small pocketbook told you to do so, you don't even know what it is to be kind, unless you are told to be." Jones' face fell a little, but she rallied admirably against his accusations.

"What's it gonna take for you to help us save your life?" She demanded. Ainsley seemed to think on this a moment.

"Ask me nicely." He offered with a graceless smile, his voice full of bitter challenge, as though he were asking her to turn against her every belief and principle with this request. Michael managed a cautious glance to the Executor; Jones' expression was blank, but her fingers gripped the edge of the desk with a fierce restraint. The room screamed with uncomfortable silence as the battle of wills was fought, and then conceded.

"Would you please, oh great Professor, help us save our reality by saving your life?" Elizabeth forced out from behind gritted teeth; defiance, insincerity and hatred coloured her tone and Ainsley smiled in the face of it. Michael held his breath in hopes that Elijah would accept the plea for the concession it was.

Ainsley jumped to his feet with a beaming smile on his face. "Well, what are we waiting for? The universe won't save itself." He opened the drawer beneath his desk and pulled all the papers and files into it before closing it with a snap. Michael turned to look at A Division, who all sighed with relief, as the pressure that had held the room throughout Elijah and Jones' strange conversation alleviated. Even the Accountant looked rattled, and he placed a comforting hand on his

Executor's shoulder. "My car's out front, and unlike yours it isn't tracked by the Ministry." Ainsley announced to the quiet room, taking his glasses off his head, and tucking them into his pocket, and with that he set off up the stairs. Michael looked between the people who had exposed his life as a lie, and the man who held them in the palm of his hand with only his demeanour and his words. He wasn't too sure who he would rather be following.

May 3rd, 1987

My C.A.L.I.G.O device is twenty years old this year. With every day that passes it becomes stronger, more powerful, and more devastating. There is now twenty years' worth of history that has been changed and moulded by the great politicians' mind and ambition. I do not remember the true flow of time, only the edited version, the version everyone accepts to be true. After all you cannot be deceived by your own recollection.

It took me a long time to figure out how the Ministry were capable of changing the very memories that existed in people's minds. It was not a technology I had blessed them with, at least so I thought. The ability to edit and change the very recollection and record of history, in some cases the personal history of people, was frightening and had the potential to cause the same level of damage that my monster could.

In true scientist fashion I took to examining the data, I reviewed the days following a successful mission. At first my focus was too small, as I soon realised that the Ministry of Time itself was not knowingly responsible for correcting the memories of the public. The first coincidence I noticed was purely by accident; in 1973 when I was still part of the Ethics Committee, I had been reviewing a mission that had gone ahead the day before. I was frustrated by my lack of recollection of the true events and had been pacing around my London flat, while a fierce freak storm raged outside. It wasn't until I was watching the news later that evening, when the weatherman recounted previous times that year in which unexpected showers and storms had occurred, that the dates began to match.

After a little research, it became clear to me that there was a direct correlation between these strange weather events and the Ministry of Time's expeditions. This was how I put correlation and causation together. I still had old blueprints and plans of my C.A.L.I.G.O device, and in reviewing them, I realised that as well as granting them the ability to change history as they saw fit, I had also granted them the ability to erase all memory to the contrary. The universe had a way of mending the damage done to it by my device and I had unwittingly turned it into a party trick.

Water was always my favourite analogy for time, after all it is not described as flowing for no reason. The truth is that time is linear like water flowing down a stream, and my device in a sense creates its own current that is circular, allowing it to return to an earlier part of the river. It cannot stop the flow, nor reverse it, only create these small whirlpools of opportunity. To generate this current, it takes a great amount of energy, this energy washes over the C.A.L.I.G.O device when it returns to its proper place in the river, as the current dissipates. The larger the changes the more energy the device required and so more energy was expelled upon its return to true time. This energy I had previously determined was not harmful and could be simply funnelled into the atmosphere to disperse.

However, I now realise that this energy, once released into the atmosphere, generates an electrical storm, which is strong enough to change electrical impulses in the mind. This is how history is changed even in the eyes of those who have lived it. This is how the universe had been healing itself from the jagged cuts I had enabled my monster to slash through its tapestry, it had healed itself through tears. It is like throwing a pebble into a river and watching the ripples. My monster forces its way through the waters of time, and in turn its ripples smooth over the damage. The universe has been course correcting as humanity tries to doom itself; we carry on, unaware of the sacrifices that are being made to redeem our sins.

I have come to hate the sound of rainfall. The fear of what has been changed; what I can no longer remember. To know that the river has been wrangled in a new direction, and the universe screams louder as the effort to stitch itself back together becomes greater with each slash to its fabric.

It was clear the Ministry had little idea about how their changes were being so readily accepted, perhaps they thought it was because they were hiding any materials that disputed what they had made of history. Whatever the reason, they had made no moves to investigate the change in memory, and arrogantly kept on hacking away at history.

When I discovered the correlation between the weather and the missions, I began breaking into the Collator's office shortly after the freak storms, to discover what it was they had changed. In doing so, I discovered why the collators had no problem remembering both true time, and that which had changed. Lead. The outer shield of my C.A.L.I.G.O device is lead, to protect its passengers from the fierce electrical surges that occur around the device by travelling through time. In the walls around the Collator's office are lead sheets protecting them from the resulting changes to their minds, although this was not the intended result as it had been done to protect against nuclear fallout.

The Ministry has always been arrogant in the face of science, believing that holding the holy grail of scientific discovery places them above it. However, it is their lack of understanding that leaves them weak. The universe has blessed me with little, except a mind that can sympathise with it, a mind that can understand its pain, and the power of destruction like a black hole. So, I can feel its pain, the pain I helped inflict, I can feel its anger. The raging of a storm beyond the Ministry of Time's comprehension, this storm runs through me. It is not an anger like fire, quick to burn and gone in a flash, it is an anger like water that builds upon itself and drowns its enemies, not leaving them time to scream.

My monster and I have suffered our deserved punishments for our crimes, and now we seek our revenge; to grant the universe the freedom it is owed. I will free it from the cage I trapped it in, that I auctioned to the highest bidder for a scrap of recognition and money. I shall swallow them like the black hole I have made of myself, like the tempestuous ocean I have become, and crush the starlight they are made from, the starlight they are undeserving of.

Professor Elijah Ainsley

Chapter 11

Ainsley pulled up outside the Ministry of Time and its dingy, dark front. Michael was relieved as he finally turned the engine off, Ainsley drove like a maniac, no doubt breaking several speeding laws and traffic warnings in the short drive. They piled out onto the pavement, where Ainsley and Jones stood waiting, ignoring each other. The Professor was gazing up at the black façade of the Ministry of Time, as though in worship. The Ministry looked far from an ornate chapel or exulting cathedral, it was not carved from marble or inlaid with precious stones as perhaps it should be. Instead, it was a nondescript grey walled building with grimy, unwashed windows that could not be looked through and a small black canopy which cast the roughened double doors into shadows. It was a perfect disguise.

Jones watched them walk towards her impassively, her back to Elijah as the man still seemed oblivious to those around him. The crowd parted and rushed around the man frozen in the middle of the pavement like a rock in a river. It had been a painful ride in silence as both Elizabeth and Elijah refused to acknowledge one another, and the remaining four of them had been too uncomfortable to try and break the silence that travelled with them like an unwelcome passenger.

Ainsley finally glanced towards them and for a moment he seemed like he had no idea where he was or who they were as he looked through them. Before Michael could ask if the Professor was alright Elijah moved towards the door and held it open with a smile. "After you." He swept his hand in an ushering motion, Elizabeth moved first, grinding her teeth as she moved past Ainsley and into the Ministry. The remaining four of them followed the Executor inside with the Professor coming in last.

The normally busy lobby was quiet, and all the corridors were on minimal lighting as though slumbering. The seemingly only other person was the receptionist, who sat as poised as ever behind the arched steel desk, typing furiously on her large clunky electric typewriter. Michael decidedly hated the technology of this time, it was unimpressive, slow, and looked far too remedial for a time in which Time Travel existed, it was also beige just like everything else in this godforsaken year.

The six of them crossed the lobby to the desk and waited for her to finish her thumping typing. She regarded each of them in turn, before addressing Jones. "What can I do for you?" She asked the Executor.
"There was a malfunction with the Excalibur Code this afternoon and we are here to escort Professor Ainsley to the device so that he can fix it." Elizabeth answered

with authority. The receptionist regarded Jones with a shrewd look.

"I have not been informed of this." She replied.

"Of course, you haven't," Jones brushed aside, "the Ministry didn't want it getting back to the MOD that there was a problem, especially seeing as we are currently under review for amendments to our funding." Jones spoke clearly and without faltering, as she lied through her teeth. "So, we shut down under the guise of an ethical issue to allow Professor Ainsley chance to fix the error. That's why it hasn't been communicated on paper." Michael had to hand it to her that she was very convincing.

"I will have to confirm this with the Director." The receptionist declared, her face the picture of scepticism as her eyes roved the Executor's features looking for any sign of falsity.

"Yes of course, however he is a busy man, and we don't have a very large window in which Professor Ainsley can fix the C.A.L.I.G.O device, so perhaps you could allow us in while you confirm?" Jones proposed, keeping all that firm authority and command in her tone. The receptionist thought on it, and cast a glance between Jones and Ainsley, who flashed her a wide, beaming grin.

"On your head be it, Agent." Then she held her hand out, waiting. Jones reached into her pocket and produced her M.O.T ID. The receptionist scanned it through and then looked back to the Agent.

"Elizabeth Jones, Executor, A Division." Elizabeth recited coolly and the receptionist nodded and returned her card. The process repeated for each member of A Division, then Elijah handed his over.

"Professor Elijah Ainsley, Genius Inventor." He said rather pompously, to everyone's surprise the receptionist nodded with a long-suffering look, as though this was a normal practice between the two of them. Then she turned a critical eye on Michael who carefully handed over his futuristic ID.

"I'm Michael Brown." He explained as she scrutinised the card. Elijah grinned at Michael with something resembling pride. She arched a brow and turned to Jones.

"He's a technician from the future. We thought he might be aware of something our own technicians aren't." Elizabeth replied to the silent question. It was a perfectly reasonable explanation, and almost ruefully the receptionist sighed in acceptance and bid them entrance.

A Division led Michael and Elijah through the twisting corridors, that looked positively uninviting in the low light. The walls were grey and bare and each one seemed identical. It felt positively apocalyptic and no matter the time of year outside it was always cold. They were no different to the halls 2005 and Michael felt that if he lingered too long the walls may start closing in. He shivered reflexively and focused on Elijah's buoyant mood that seemed unaffected by the unpleasant surroundings.

Eventually, they arrived at the Time Hall and were met with the awesome sight of the C.A.L.I.G.O device in all its glory. Michael knew then that he would never get over what it is to look upon the time machine. Each time he saw it, he was filled with this sense of something beyond the ordinary purview, something that shouldn't be, but was. The low light reflected off the grey-blue metal casting beautiful shadows across the machines swooping planes. The device stood on its point as though perfectly balanced. It was a technology that was dreamt and wildly theorised about, made real. This time though, he stood next to its enigmatic creator, who had defied the laws of both nature and man to pull the device from the ether, where it had flitted out of reach.

Michael managed to tear his gaze from the device to look at Elijah, who to his surprise seemed to be on the brink on tears. "It has been a long time since I stood this close to my device." He said quietly. The four agents looked slightly ashamed at his words, to Michael's confusion. The creator walked slowly towards his device, as though he thought it might disappear before his crystal blue eyes. He stretched his hand out to caress the lead casing, and a true smile crept onto his face when it didn't dematerialise beneath his touch. "It's good to see you, my monster." Michael frowned but did not comment on the strange affection.

"Well, what are we waiting for?" The Professor span back to them, his sombre, melancholic mood gone in a flash and replaced with a manic energy. "Christopher, I believe you are going to need some weapons if you intend to kill my would-be assassin. Miss Thomas, your expertise will surely be needed, and I suggest you find a Chameleon case." He then turned to the Executor, the Historian and the Technician who were watching him with bewilderment. "And I'm going to need you three to help me jump start C.A.L.I.G.O, so come on, chop chop." He clapped his hands together and reluctantly Stevens and Thomas left to carry out their tasks.

"Right Charlie," The Historian looked entirely discomfited by Elijah's use of his nickname. "I need you to head over to the generator in the corner and give it a good wind up, the Ministry's running on little power at the moment, so we need to make our own." Morris nodded and dragged himself over to the large generator. He was by far the least enthusiastic one of them and Michael couldn't work out why. It was as though the Historian was physically weighed down.

"Michael," Michael snapped his attention back to Ainsley. "I need you to get up in the crow's nest and set all the levels to zero to begin a manual engagement." Michael nodded and quickly moved over to the ladder to pull himself up to the caged control centre. He flicked all the switches down, twisted all the knobs back to their lowest position and reduced all the voltage faders to zero. He looked down to see Jones blockading the door with desks and chairs, as Elijah moved under the C.A.L.I.G.O device with two jump leads.

"Michael down here!" He looked down, to see one jump lead being offered to him, he took it from Ainsley, careful to keep the metal away from himself and the control desk. "Attach it to the electrode at the back of you." Michael turned and clipped it to the copper pipe that ended in a large ball above him.
"It's on!" He called down to Ainsley.
"Good, now keep your hand on the master voltage control. When I give you the signal you need to turn it all the way up, understand?"
"Yeah, I got it!" He called back and rested his hand over the large control. He turned as he heard someone climbing the ladder. Jones appeared and stood to the left of him. Michael found himself suddenly unnerved by her presence and drummed his spare hand on his leg in agitation.

Across the room, Morris was still winding, and Elijah had made his way over to him to watch the power gauge tick up on the generator.
"How's this supposed to work Ainsley?" Jones asked from across the hall.

"My device stores energy as part of its return protocol, and releases what it cannot hold into the atmosphere. Which means its battery is always full, even if you pull the plug, and so to start up the control desk and allow it to travel, the only thing we need to do is give it a little kick, and it should have more than enough power to do what we need it to do."
"Should have?" The Executor asked sceptically.
"You can trust me when it comes to science Agent Jones, I am a mad scientist at heart, and this is my device. I know it better and more intimately than anyone else could ever hope to." He said with nothing, but amusement present in his voice. "Alright, you ready Michael?"
"Yeah, all ready on your signal."
"Okay on three..." Ainsley knelt down to the circuit breaker release, "One... Two... Three!" He pulled the release and Michael turned the knob all the way up. Nothing happened for a moment, then above his head a large crackle of lightning snapped from the copper ball to the smaller zinc ball that sat on top of the C.A.L.I.G.O device. The device gave a great shudder and then the control desk lit up with life, and the dials flicked up in answer. Michael found himself laughing, they'd just managed to jump start a time machine like you would a car.

There was the sound of someone climbing the ladder, he and Jones looked to see the crazy inventor himself grinning wildly. He made his way to the control panel, pulling out his glasses as he did so, setting the frames on his face to cover his discerning blue-grey eyes, as he set about correcting the dials and quantities. Michael found himself admiring the quick way the creator moved over the knobs and gauges, he was like a brilliant composer before an orchestra of numbers and calculations.

"You're really good at this." Jones murmured, and only seemed to realise she'd said it aloud when both Michael and Elijah looked to her. Elijah huffed a laugh of genuine amusement.
"What? Good at secretly jump starting my device? Or subverting the wishes of the Ministry of Time?" He asked, returning to his composing.
"You know I had to report you." She reminded as though this was an age-old argument between them. He paused again and his curls hung in front of his bowed face.
"Perhaps, but either way, you're the reason I haven't been allowed to even step foot in this building without an escort for three years." He stood straight and regarded her. "The only reason we got past the receptionist at the door was because you turned against me before, and so she had very little concern about allowing me near my device if you are here with me." That bitter smile crept back onto his face. "Because all of the M.O.T know that the slippery Professor Ainsley can't get away with anything if the great Executor Jones is in the building." Cruelty was etched into his face now, like it had always been a part of him. "Tell me, did you

at least get a decent pay rise out of it? Or was it simply because you like being the Director's favourite?"

Michael had a flash back to a similar conversation and accusation he'd been party to not hours ago, a conversation that wouldn't take place until nearly thirty years in the future. Hurt flashed across her face, before it was replaced by that defiance she wore like armour around Ainsley.
"You were stealing files. What happened to you is not my fault, any other Agent would have reported you." With that, she turned and climbed down from the crow's nest.

Michael kept silent as Ainsley began turning dials again, much slower than before. The Professor sighed and stared at his device. His face was illuminated from beneath by the control panel, which cast dark shadows over the planes of his profile, causing his usually blue eyes to fade to grey. "She's right of course, but she doesn't yet see the corruption that lives at the heart of the great Ministry of Time, and someone has to know what is being changed, especially the changes that aren't being put to the Ethics Committee."
"You know they're changing things without approval of the Ethics Committee?" Michael asked, astounded. Elijah laughed.
"Of course, they are, and why wouldn't they?" He shook his head ruefully. "They can make history the way they want it to be, give themselves as much power as they

could dream of. It helps, that no one ever remembers what has been changed, as we only remember history as we have been told it happened. It was my worst mistake handing this weapon to these politicians."

Chapter 12

Michael was sat on an abandoned office chair, examining the contents of his wallet, all his credit cards were now irrelevant, but on the bright side he wouldn't have to pay any of them off. "Here." Stevens' voice interrupted his thoughts; he looked up to see the suited man offering him his gun. It was clearly more modern than the Accountant's own; Michael didn't really know why he had taken the gun; he had no idea how to use it and it was wasted on him.
"I'm not the greatest shot, maybe it's better if you take mine, it's a little more advanced than your own." Stevens looked down at the gun in consideration, before raising it as though aiming down the sight. Then to Michael's surprise, he fired it. It made an almighty bang in the large hall, and all the other occupants ducked in fright.
"Hmmm, it's a nice gun." Stevens said as though they were in a practice range and not in a room with a lot of highly temperamental, expensive, and calibrated equipment.

"Christ, give everyone a bit of warning, would you?" Ainsley shouted down at the two of them.
"Sorry." Stevens called back. "Alright you've got a deal, but you should still take mine in case of an emergency." He offered out the older looking handgun, which Michael took tentatively as his ears were still ringing and Stevens had just proven himself highly unpredictable, especially for an Accountant.

"What the hell was that? You could have just given us away?" Jones demanded as she squared up to her second.
"They almost certainly already know that your excuse was a lie, and that we have just allowed the mad creator who hates this institution to access his time machine, if they think we're armed it'll make them think twice." The Accountant's frightening logic ended the argument, and he held out another gun to his Executor. Jones, Michael was starting to learn hated losing arguments, as evidenced by the glare she levelled at her Accountant, who was unconcerned by the fiery gaze.

The six of them congregated before the steps to the gangplank. Michael looked around at their strange group; Alison held a briefcase in front of her legs, and the rest of them carried handguns, even the Professor, who to everyone's surprise knew how to use it perfectly. "So, I suppose the obvious question is who is staying behind?" Ainsley asked of the five of them.

Michael braced himself for them to tell him he was to guard the door.

"I am." Came the voice of Charles Morris. They all turned to look at him in confusion, all but Ainsley.

"I don't have a black book. Not for this, but you all do, and so it's clear someone made the choice a long time ago that it was you four." Michael blinked in shock, he hadn't realised that Charlie didn't have a black book, he had assumed that all of A Division had received them for this mission, but apparently not. "Besides, I'd rather not know what happens if it's all the same to you. My heads already full of so many conflicting timelines, events, and morality that I don't want to know anymore." Alison laid a comforting hand on his arm. Michael finally realised then what the terrible burden was that plagued the Historian, to know the true flow of time, and to have to be retold all of humanities failure each week, just as you have blissfully forgotten them.

Elijah looked like he wasn't particularly happy with that arrangement but did not object. "Alright Mr Morris and I will stay behind and guard the door for as long as we can, but I suggest you do not dally in 1967. If they recall the C.A.L.I.G.O device, you will be 'Timeless' like our Mr Brown here, and I doubt any of you would take it as well as he has." He gave them all a scolding look. "Now, my workshop is where the Collator's office is now, and that is where you will find me and my assassin. Michael?" He asked.

"Yeah?"

"What is the margin of error on the 2005 device?"

"It's plus or minus three minutes and forty-one seconds." He recalled, remembering giving his own lecture that morning.

"Impressive," Ainsley remarked with a considering tilt of his head, "this device unfortunately is plus or minus five minutes and sixteen seconds, so even if I send you back to the same point it's likely he's got a head start." A Division nodded and made to move for the time capsule.

"Wait just a moment." Elijah sighed. "There's something else you need to know. I have studied Time Travel for most of my life, and what I have learnt is that great Time Travel, when done correctly, leaves no ripples behind. It is seamless and perfect and does not leave a gaping hole in our reality. I am counting on you to ensure there is no ripples from your travels. That means no big changes to the flow of events alright?" He asked sternly. "It will also ensure the Ministry cannot track what you have done, do you understand?" His face the image of a general giving grim orders to grim troops. They nodded. "Good. I did not create my device to rip holes in Time, I created it to slip seamlessly between the fabric of reality. I don't want to be responsible for any more damage, I have done enough already." With that dark statement he left the group and beckoned Michael over to him.

"Here, you left this in my office." He held out Michael's black book between them. Michael was truly surprised, in all his life he had never gone a period of time without knowing where the small pocketbook was, but he had abandoned it in Ainsley's lecture hall without a thought. "Maybe have a look at it when you think of me?" Ainsley asked with a smile on his face, his blue eyes twinkling with amusement. Michael mirrored it and took the book from him.

The two men looked over to A Division, where Charlie had paused a moment to say his goodbyes to his team. "I'll see you in 1967 then." Ainsley said clapping his hand on Michael's shoulder, but unlike the last person who had done so, there was no lingering weight left for Michael to carry. Together Elijah and Charlie climbed up to the crow's nest and the remaining four of them climbed the steps to the gangplank. They each entered the capsule and the hatch hissed shut behind them. There was no turning back now.

September 27th, 1990

I have been set on this path of revenge for several years now, and even when it was not my intention to be aligned against the interests of the Ministry of Time, I found myself stood against them anyway. I have been called deliberately argumentative and contrary many times, especially in my time as a member of the Ethics Committee. Which I think speaks more of their morals than of my own. As you have seen, morality has never been of much consequence to me. I think I discovered too early on that morality is too interchangeable, too nebulous, and too easily bought to be worth anything. It was clear to me, or so I thought, that science is amoral; science is neither good nor bad, it is simply progression. It is only granted a type of morality by those who use it, and for the purpose they seek from it.

I have often referred to my invention as a monster, but it is not strictly true. My device is a reflection of me, and I am not fond of mirrors or metaphors that cast me in a bad light. Yet, while I now accept the monstrous qualities I possess, the cruelty I see in my creation is not a reflection of me, I know I am not cruel at the heart of myself. We are all capable of cruelty and I am no exception, but it is not my tendency to be cruel. Naïve? Yes, but not naturally cruel. No, I think the cruelty I see in my device is mirrored from those who have abused it. I created it with the intention of preventing suffering, and perhaps even generating happiness, as a way for others to visit those they have lost. The Ministry have used my creation to further their own ends and ambitions and, in some cases, inflict more suffering upon humanity where there should have been none.

Like Frankenstein, my monster is innocent, it reflects only that which we see in ourselves and in our fellow men. Enlightened as I fear myself to be, I recognise what must be done to free our free will, and to do so I must make use of the monster in me to do things others would call immoral. At least that is what I must force myself to believe as I encourage others to suffer and sacrifice for my mistakes, to redeem this humanity we are so proud to be a part of.

Today is one of those instances I must convince myself of my convoluted philosophies, as I approach a young innocent boy and ask him to sacrifice everything for my sake. It is his tenth birthday, a large landmark in any young child's life as he enters double figures and stands on the precipice of beginning his journey into a young adult. He is happier than I remember him being. It makes it all so much harder. This is why the universe allowed me all I have taken from it, so that I can carry out this purpose right here. I am the black hole for a reason, the monster in the dark for this reason and if I don't fulfil it, my life has no reason at all, and nothing I have ever done is worth anything.

He is small, and his bright blonde hair shines in the dying summer sun, he is the very centre of a supernova. He looks up at me in surprise, but there is no fear in his sparkling, icy blue eyes, even though I can see the monster I am reflected in his eyes. I take the black book out of my pocket in shaking hands, I stole this book from a brilliant young man many years ago, a man long dead. A man I am dooming to his fate in this moment.

The boy carefully takes the book from me, wonder in his eyes, as he believes it a gift. I cannot walk away without saying goodbye. I thank him. This young child deserves an apology, but I am not a good enough man to give him one, so I thank him for his service and force myself to leave his path. I am the first of many monsters he will meet, but I refuse to be the one to break him. Not now. Not when he can still have a semblance of a life.

I have ruined his life. It is the only thought I am capable of. I have ruined his life, but the universe won't scream for him when he collapses. No, it will not. It has made him for this purpose after all, he is made to be a sacrifice to redeem the mistakes of men who will never give him a second glance. It is perhaps this act that will truly and forever damn me beyond comprehension, there is no starlight waiting for me.

Professor Elijah Ainsley, Ph. D

Chapter 13

The C.A.L.I.G.O device juddered to a halt, and Michael felt like he was going to throw up. He'd thought that the 2005 device had bad stability, but the 1977 model was like a fairground ride that spun its occupants around like a washing machine. Jones grinned at the obvious green hue in his face. "Nothing like Time Travel." She said, clearly holding back laughter as Michael shakily unclipped himself from the Historian's seat.

Stevens opened the hatch, and Michael shuffled out onto the gangplank after A Division. "Okay, this is weird." Alison announced to them. The Half- Way Hall was only halfway finished, the walls were unpainted and industrial beams were exposed, wires lay about the floor and scaffolds stood on one side of the room.
"Of course, it's weird, the Ministry doesn't exist yet." The Executor said to her Chameleon.

The Accountant checked his watch, "We're a minute and twenty-three seconds late, and clearly our competition is already here." They looked to see the other docking bay occupied by the 2005 device. They were in fixed time now. "We need to move."

The four of them took off at a sprint through the not quite Ministry of Time. There was a difference Michael noted, between himself now and the version of him that had been itching to get ready for the assassins' appearance. The deep-seated fear of being late that had been present was now no longer so. Now, it was like time was moving with him rather than against him.

Ahead, Stevens and Jones took ahold of their guns and Michael reached for his own. They skidded to a halt outside what would be the double door entrance to the

Collators office. Christopher held his hand up in a halting motion, as he listened in at the door. Michael flicked the safety off the old, yet modern weapon. In a flash, Stevens was in the doorway, with Jones at his side, both with their guns raised. Michael moved with them, holding his gun in the direction of the two men already in the room.

Kneeling with his back to them, was a young Elijah Ainsley. Stood facing them was his assassin, with his handgun aimed straight at Ainsley's forehead. Behind the pair of them was an unfinished C.A.L.I.G.O device, that loomed over the assassin and his victim alike, like an omen of death.

His assassin was familiar now that he had removed his face covering, and Michael stiffened as he recognised the much older face of Charlie Morris holding the universe at gunpoint. Next to him he saw the Executor's aim waver in realisation and the Accountant clench his jaw.
"Ah I wondered if I might see you." Came the gruff voice of the once Historian and close friend. "I hoped that I would, but then I have a rather negative idea of Michael's competence, having of course already met him as the idiot who managed to get himself 'Timeless' in 1977."
"You don't have to do this Charlie." Alison pleaded from his left; the first of them to recover their ability to speak.

"I know that, Ali. Unlike you lot I'm actually capable of making decisions without the aid of a black book." Charlie goaded. Christopher ignored his derision and tried to appeal to logic.

"Think about what this will do to the world. You will create an unsustainable paradox, that could rip apart the fabric of reality." The Accountant reminded him. Charlie laughed in the face of his words, as though Stevens was being particularly dim.
"Of course, it will, but he deserves it! You don't know what they've done in the future! How they've taken away free will with this accursed device and manipulated everything in the favour of those more 'deserving'!" He sneered the last part. "And they can only do this because of this one man's selfish ambition! He has to die! Because he will poison our world and turn it into his personal playground!" He screamed in Elijah's face.

It was only then that Michael was aware that Elijah was speaking. "I'm sorry, so sorry! You have to forgive me! I'm sorry please!" he whispered to his murderer. Michael's anger rose in him, what the Ministry had done with Ainsley's device was not his fault.
"Nothing you can say will change my mind." Charlie whispered back to his victim. "The world will thank me." He assured himself, "Goodbye Mr Ainsley."
"Charlie wait!" Jones yelled; too late.

The gun fired, and Professor Elijah Ainsley slumped to the floor. Michael felt time slow. The murderer raised his gun at Michael, who could not respond, frozen in the moment of their failure. Two further shots sounded, muffled, and the murderer fell too, to the floor beside his victim.

Michael rushed forward to the body of one of the greatest men who ever lived. The great inventor laid prone; his curly dark hair fell around his head like a halo, as his usually all-seeing eyes stared glassily up to the heavens. In the centre of his forehead a perfectly circular hole trickled a stream of blood down the left side of his face, the edges of the hole were burnt black. Slowly blood began to pool around the back of his head, sluggish and staining. Michael wasn't even aware of Jones, Stevens, or Thomas, only his friend, who he had failed. The first person who had ever believed in him, who had trusted him to save his life. He was too late, too slow, and too useless to have ever saved Ainsley's life.

On shaky hands he pushed himself to his feet, swallowing back bile as his head felt like it had ruptured open. The universe would end any moment now, and Michael would welcome it with open arms, he wished for death, for numb mindless eternity. To be free of the pain that ravaged his pounding head in the wake of his failure. Time could not collapse quick enough.

Michael cast a brief disgusted look at Elijah's murderer. He had been right. Michael would realise the truth, the truth that he is nothing more than the wrong brother, the useless technician, who achieved nothing in all twenty-four years of his life and failed at the one thing he had promised to do. Then he would die, as the universe collapsed in on itself, unable to mend itself from Michael's mistake.

Guiltily he looked for comfort in these last moments, searching for those brilliant blue eyes full of a tempestuous ocean, that reflected the tapestry of the universe. He looked down into brown eyes, and realised they were not the eyes he was looking for. They were the wrong colour. Warm honeyed brown stared up at Michael where there should have a fierce icy blue.

Breath returned to him, as he thought back to the clear pale blue eyes that had comforted him in his anguish, eyes that were more familiar than he had first recognised, because they were the eyes he had seen in the mirror, for twenty-four years of sacrifice. With trembling fingers, he reached into his pocket and pulled out a black book that was not quite his.

October 16th, 1999

I find that I have missed the limelight in my seclusion from the outside world, and so when I was offered the opportunity to be the centre of attention once again, I could hardly deny it. Not as I sit in the knowledge it will not be something I will be able to do in the coming years. Not with my choice of revenge. If my plan comes to fruition the world shall know the truth behind C.A.L.I.G.O and the Ministry alike; my first true act of free will in my long life shall be to destroy my own creation. A fitting end.

Looking back at the miserable experience that has been my life, there was only a small period in which I was ever slightly happier, and that was when I was a teacher. In some ways, I feel it is probably my true calling. I have a tendency to speak at people, rather than to them, and I have always enjoyed knowing things others do not, watching the look of amazement on their faces when I let them in on the secret. Knowledge about our universe, about our history should never be denied or hidden from view, or God forbid changed. For this reason, teaching has always been my guilty pleasure.

This is how I ended up in my old lecture hall with a packed room. To my amazement people have filled the walkways, they crowd the doors hoping to listen in, they sit crossed legged on the floor, establishing a new front row. They sit in an admiring silence, enraptured by my every word, barely allowing themselves to blink as I talk of the universe, the secrets it harbours and the ones we have left to discover.

It is strange I think, to be a black hole and be admired by the stars, the planets, and the great expanse itself.

I look up into the rafters, and with ease I find the supernova that remains incandescent despite me. His blonde hair has dulled somewhat and curls around his ears, as he can't afford too many haircuts on his student loan. He watches me closer than any other, with cool blue eyes alight with amazement as though I am the centre of his universe as he is the centre of mine. To him nothing I say is a surprise, the universe has already told him all its secrets, and he will need all of them to survive his future that he will find in the past. He is not the young man I met in this room over two decades ago. He is not the man I drunk whiskey with, as we discussed the fine philosophy upon which our universe sits. He will become that man, and he will meet a much younger version of me, who will become the man who stands in front of him now and talks of the wonders that can be found in our vast universe.

After all, he has already undergone much change from the baby whose birthday I toasted as the most important man to ever be born, to the child whose life I ruined with a small black pocketbook, to the young man who watches now from amidst the galaxy around him. Michael Brown has much left to change, and to be changed by, but in all this he remains the most brilliant man I ever knew, and that will not change.

Professor Elijah Ainsley, Ph. D, Godfather of Time Travel.

Chapter 14

Michael looked up to Jones, Stevens, and Thomas, who were still bent over the body of the once great inventor. The great inventor, who was not the same one they knew in '77. The despair that warps their features feels already like a distant memory to Michael. For they don't understand. He couldn't help but laugh at the ridiculousness of his situation.
"What?" Elizabeth asked distantly, her tone crippled with misery and despondency.
"We didn't fail." Michael said through giggles. Stevens gave him a concerned look, like Michael was being particularly slow.
"Ainsley's dead, of course we failed." Alison enunciated slowly.
"Yes, *that* Ainsley's dead, but that isn't the same man that calls himself Elijah Ainsley in the future." Michael explained.

Stevens frowned then dropped his gaze to the black book in Michael's hand. Ever the logician he looked to

the glassy brown eyes of the victim, before looking up into the blue eyes he knew to be Professor Ainsley's.
"You're going to take his place?" Christopher asked, disbelief in his voice. Michael nodded.
"I already have, no ripples remember."

Michael was sat atop a trunk full of tools, as Alison brushed permanent hair dye into his dull blond locks. It had the same consistency of water and was unlike any hair dye he had ever seen, as it soaked into his scalp. He was obediently chewing a keratin supplement that would grow his hair out to a similar length of that of Ainsley's over the next couple of minutes. "Alright that's enough, spit." She held out a small bowl in front of his face, and he rid himself of the decidedly unpleasant tasting chewing gum.

He could tell that she was the most unsettled by the revelation of Charlie's betrayal, gone was the kindly disposition she had sported in all their acquaintance, and instead a forced calm had taken over her. She reached into her brief case and produced a small pill. "This'll give you a slight tan, enough to pass yourself off as Ainsley, who has spent the last few months in an underground workshop. You need to swallow that one." She handed it over to him with a bottle of water. Michael knocked it back and stared up at her as she considered his appearance. She sighed. "You're also gonna need to eat a lot over the next couple of weeks, because you're far too skinny to be Ainsley." Her eyes fell critically on the large plaster on his forehead. "That you'll have to pass off as a work accident." Michael nodded in understanding.

Stevens and Jones re-entered the workshop, having disposed of the bodies of both murderer and victim. Jones was carrying a full mop and bucket, while Stevens held a large bottle of bleach. Michael cast a glance over to the two pools of blood under the shadow of the Time Machine, which had only just begun to swirl together. Together the Executor and her Accountant began scrubbing the blood stains away, erasing the true flow of events. Alison returned to his field of vision holding what looked like an oiling rag. "Tip your head forward." She commanded. Michael tipped forward, letting his sopping wet hair fall in his eyes, something it would not have been long enough to do a few moments ago. The Chameleon set to drying it roughly, and Michael endured it.

When it was sufficiently dry, she pushed him back upright and reached for Ainsley's wallet, that they had stolen from him. She produced the dead Elijah's driving license and examined the photograph in comparison to Michael's new likeness. "It's sufficient." She declared before reaching back into her briefcase and taking out a Polaroid camera. "Take off the plaster and hold still." Michael reached up and tentatively pulled the plaster off, trying not to wince; Alison stepped forward and pulled a dark lock of hair over the wound. Carefully, she lined up the border of the photo with the style of a passport profile. She snapped it once, taking the printed image, along with the driving license over to a technical drawing board.

Finally left alone, Michael pulled out his new black book. To his surprise it only detailed the next ten years of his life, only instructing him up to October 6th, 1977, with the last command being to retire from society. Another ten years of following orders, but this time the choice to follow them would be his own and once they were up, he would be able to do as he pleased. Just ten more years and free will would finally be his. He flipped back to the front and reviewed his commands for next hour. It felt strange to be learning a new script, to hold a black book and not know every word by heart.

"You okay?" The cool voice of Christopher Stevens interrupted his thoughts. Michael looked up.
"Yeah, fine." This was met with unvoiced scepticism, but otherwise accepted.
"Here." Stevens held out his watch. Tentatively, Michael took it from him. "It automatically syncs itself to the Atomic Clock." Sure enough, on its face it gave the current date of June 22nd, 1967, of precisely four minutes and forty-one seconds past three in the afternoon.
"Thank you." Michael said sincerely, attaching it to his wrist. He looked down at his ruffled and dirty clothes, it had been the longest day, and there were still things

that needed to be said and done. He stood and brushed his trousers down. "I think you should go now." He announced. "The Ministry will be undoubtedly trying to break into the 'Time Hall' by now, and Elijah and Charlie can't hold them off forever."
"No." Came Elizabeth's instant denial. "We can stay a bit longer."
"No, you can't." Michael replied waving his black book, in imitation of her in their first conversation, and Ainsley several years from now. "You have to go and let me finish the C.A.L.I.G.O device." He saw the moment he won the argument, as Lizzie's face fell, and she glared at the floor. It would likely be the only time he would ever win an argument with her so easily, he struggled to find that amusing.

"You also need to leave me your black books so that I can give them to your younger selves." With the three of them still reeling from the betrayal of their friend they were all surprisingly compliant. Without argument, all three of them handed over their pocketbooks; Alison handed over his now edited Driving License.
"What if someone close to Elijah realises you aren't him?" Stevens asked, his gaze on the forged ID.
"All of Elijah's family are dead at this point in his life, he has no close friends and has spent close to six months down in this workshop alone. I'd say it's unlikely." Michael recited from his study of Ainsley's life. His life now. He took a deep breath as the weight of this new

history settled on his shoulders. "Come on, I'll walk you out."

Three hours later the first fully functional, life sustaining Time Travel machine was completed by Elijah Ainsley.

August 9th, 2005

This shall be my final entry to you, as I imagine the police will soon be breaking down my door on charges of treason and crimes against the state. The world knows now that the Ministry of Time exists, and that they have been using my device to change history as they see fit. The world knows now that the last thirty-eight years are a lie, and that the British Government have held its people hostage to their whims, keeping the most powerful weapon ever created, secret from its allies and enemies alike. For that's the practical use of my device. A weapon for a new age. A weapon responsible for loss of life, potential, and a history to be proud of.

Today, I finally unchained free will from where it was trapped in the depths of the politicians' pockets. It is also the culmination of my actions that were not dictated by a small black book. Today, I do not have to be Professor Elijah Ainsley, Ph. D, Godfather of Time Travel, but I can be who I should have been from the beginning, the young man who burnt as bright as a supernova. Now the universe can rest, it does not have to scream as it is torn apart by my creation and its cruel masters, it does not have to stitch its tapestry of marvels back together.

I will never be full of starlight again, and that is my punishment for my younger foolishness, but being a black hole is not so bad, everything must come to end, all stars must die. I, however, did not die when my light was taken from me, no, instead I embraced the change and in doing so I have become the kind of God I always dreamed of being. A God the universe can accept and be used to crush those foolish god-like men who dare challenge it. It seems I got what I always wanted. Perhaps it does not look like I thought it would, but I am content with it all the same.

I imagine you understand who I am now. Elijah Ainsley died on June 22nd, 1967, a smart man to be sure, but a fool. However, the universe needed him to live, so that it might have a future in which the ploys of men do not torture their creator so. I took his place, his identity, his life, like a cuckoo, and I gave up my life to do so. I surrendered my starlight and became the black hole the universe needed, to take the light from those who do not deserve it. This I did without hope of a reward, without recognition.

I hope that the world has the common sense to not destroy my creation, but to remember it for the lesson it is. I hope it stands proudly in a museum as a relic, and testament to the foolishness of humanity. Perhaps I shall get a little accreditation, not as this persona, but as I truly am.

I must leave you now as I can hear the sirens. I hope you can learn from my mistakes and live your lives in the light of the universe, whether that be as your very own star, or as the swathes of space that graciously allow others to shine. Though if you do not, I hope you take with you the grave warning I must impart upon you, if it has not been made clear, there are black holes in the great expanse, and they destroy all in their path, they will come for you. They are not individuals but were once supernovas who collapsed in a bow of surrender to the universe.

Michael Brown
AKA Professor Elijah Ainsley 1967-2005

Chapter 15

Elijah cast a glance to the door, where Charlie Morris was trying to hold the blockade in place to prevent the Ministry officials from breaking into the Time Hall. "Where are they?" The murderer shouted to him. It had

been very strange spending the last few hours with the man who would later become the assassin trying to kill him. Well not quite him. Elijah glanced down at his watch; the one Christopher will return without.
"Shouldn't be too long now!" He called back. He willed the tearful farewell along.

He remembered now how the three agents praised him for his bravery and sacrifice. How they had promised to keep the memory of Michael Brown alive. He remembered their silent respect, a far cry from the derision and hate that had brimmed in their eyes when confronted with him over the last few years. He could admit, if only to himself that he had only riled and teased them as he had because he had felt so angry and alone in the last decade. They had promised to remember him, and they had not, could not. Logically, he understood that they had yet to experience the events that he could recall so clearly, but it did not make the anger any less fierce, or his brittle sanity any easier to hold onto. So, he had made them remember him as he was now, the bitter creator who was spiteful, prideful, and so full of fury it was a wonder he wasn't incandescent with it. He had fallen into the role so deeply he had no idea what seeing them, with all the weight of the history between them, would feel like.

Elijah looked down at his watch again. It was time. He looked down at the control desk, beneath his hands the dials flicked up in recognition of the impending

C.A.L.I.G.O device. "Now!" He yelled to Charlie, who abandoned his post and sprinted for the crow's nest's protection. With his murderer was safely beside him, Elijah twisted the power buffers allowing for a cushioned landing. Electricity crackled from above, striking the point in space where the C.A.L.I.G.O should be. Once, twice, thrice. Before the device snapped into its proper place in time.

He grinned at his monster, in its presence it felt like the universe itself had coalesced into the beautiful machine. Even now it was his, its presence felt like something otherworldly. The hatch hissed open, and Elijah braced himself. A loud bang came from his left, as the Ministry broke down the blockade and streamed into the room, guns held aloft focusing on the trespassers. Beside him Charlie raised his hands, Elijah finished the final landing adjustments on the control panel. If everything had gone as it should, the Ministry would not be able to work out where they had gone. Not that they would be able to change anything, after all it was fixed time now. He looked up to see the three agents stepping out of the capsule, arms raised in surrender, each one of them staring at him, that old, yet new respect in their gazes.

Lizzie's gaze caused him to finally freeze. That defiance she had armoured herself with, around him was gone. In its place was anger, but not anger against him, but rather for him. It was the strangest thing. He held her stare and felt a small smile of relief creep onto his face. It was nice to be finally understood, finally seen for who he was, and that was certainly not the same person he liked to call himself. His concentration was broken as Ministry agents crested the crow's nest and bent his arms down and behind his back to clap him in handcuffs. He took a breath and allowed that smug façade to return, like slipping back beneath the water, it was not over just yet.

Elijah was escorted to the front desk by his two delightful interrogators of the last ten hours. The Ministry of Time was awash with Time agents, engineers, and other superlative Ministry of Defence employees, in their drab unremarkable office attire. Professor Ainsley was pleased however, to see the secretive glances cast his way, and the more blatant stares by some younger staff. It was good to know he could still command the attention of the ordinary people. He tried not to let his appreciation show too much.

The young receptionist sat behind the steel desk; she looked up at their arrival. She appeared rather harried, unlike the cool professionalism that usually cloaked her. There was a sense of awe and disbelief in her eyes as she took Elijah in first, before regarding his escorts in turn.
"Mr Ainsley- "

"Professor Ainsley." Elijah cut in, leaning his elbow on the desk, and casting his best bemused look of superiority, at the faceless suited man, he even cocked his head to finish the image off. The man paused before correcting himself.
"Professor Ainsley is here to turn in his official M.O.T key card, and to have his access code log in stricken from the database. Professor Ainsley will only have access to the Ministry of Time should he be escorted by a person of Alpha clearance or higher." Throughout the suits' performative speech, he kept perfect eye contact with Elijah, it was unusual, and Elijah gave him credit for it.

Ainsley sighed, holding his hands up, as if in surrender, before facing the stoic desk woman, he flashed her a defeated smile, before procuring his wallet and tugging out the appropriate card. He slapped it on the steel surface and winked to her as he turned back to his escorts.
"Now gentlemen, as lovely as this has been, I have a lecture at nine and it's just gone eight, so I shall leave you to your jobs. Thank you ever so much for helping me to the exit, it has been delightful getting to know you both." Elijah clapped the vocal Ministry man on his shoulder, who glared at the offending hand, as though Ainsley had wiped horse shit on his perfectly pressed suit. In reply, the Professor only tightened his hand and his smile, before striding between the two suits, basking

in all the lovely stares that followed him out the building.

On the street outside, London had woken up, and the pavements were bustling with commuters, all of whom ignored him and the nondescript building that housed the weapon that could potentially change every aspect of who they thought they were. Ainsley took a deep breath, acclimatising himself to the mundane once again. Gone was the sparkling power and brilliance that came from being around his device, and now he was exiled to this other world of wind-up windows and brick like phones. It was times like this he missed his Nokia. No. He wasn't to think of that. That was not a kind of thought Professor Elijah Ainsley, Genius, Godfather of Time Travel would have. Elijah shook his head and moved to his Ford Cortina.

He flicked his key out of his pocket and went to unlock the door before he sighed and saw the parking ticket that was stuck under his windscreen wiper.
"Michael." Came a voice to his left. He froze. It had been a long time since he'd been addressed by that name.
Elizabeth Jones stood about a metre from him, her face unlike anything he had ever seen. Sadness swam in her features. For a moment they stood watching each other. Then Michael remembered his purpose.

"I've been excommunicated from M.O.T, there's not much I can do to help you from now on." He focused on being practical. "You can't ever tell Charlie. And you mustn't ever treat him any different. He must come to his own conclusions, and act accordingly. He's not wrong, but that doesn't mean his actions are right." He slid the key in the door and pulled it open. "And you must regain the M.O.T's trust, continue your missions, and live your life as if you don't know the truth." He forced himself to make eye contact with her, "I'm sorry." Then finally he turned from her, childish emotion was clawing its way up his throat making it hard to talk, and he felt twenty-four again. He clambered into his car, clicking the door shut behind him. The car's shell muffled the outside world as he stared forward. He was so alone.

There came a knock on his window. At first, he made no move to acknowledge it, Michael didn't think he could face Lizzie right now, not between characters like this. He had no idea how she wanted him to react, and no idea how he was supposed to react. The soft knock came again. He just didn't want to be alone, was that so bad?

He wound the window down a crack and forced his gaze to the gap. A manilla folder was held through it. Not what he had been expecting. Carefully he took ahold of it and read the title.
'God Save The Queen – Sex Pistols

No.1 1977'

"You are not alone Ainsley, not anymore." For the first time in over ten years Michael could have wept. He looked up, but Lizzie was gone. A small smile crept onto his face, completely without his control, he set the file down on the passenger seat, before finally starting the car.

He had only a week before he finally claimed his reward. One week before finally he would have free will, and then the Ministry of Time had better be prepared, for he was coming for them. Michael Brown was coming for them.

Epilogue

Elizabeth Jones, the most famed Executor to ever work for the Ministry of Time, strode into the crumbling organisation. That morning the Police had discovered the origin of the exposé and had tracked the IP address to a country mansion belonging to one Professor Elijah Ainsley, genius inventor and recluse. It was on every tv channel, in every language, in every country, as the world awaited the capture of both the man who stole their free will, and the man who gave it back to them. If that wasn't a god, Elizabeth didn't know what was. The Ministry of Time was in chaos as police officers, government officials, and secret service agents ran through its corridors. In all the disorder no one even noticed Jones as she strode with purpose down the once hallowed halls.

She made her way through the maze of the Ministry and into the Time Hall that lay at the centre. Of course, the other reason for the lack of security, was that the C.A.L.I.G.O device that now sat in the Ministry of Time was completely useless. The 'Excalibur code' that allowed people to survive in the time capsule had been stolen, and the last people to be in the presence of the device were either missing or had been found tied up in the corner of the hall. The dead C.A.L.I.G.O device sat quietly in its dock as though it was finally at rest, it no longer emanated an otherworldly feeling it seemed tangible now, an impressive feat of engineering to be sure but a godly weapon no more.

In the centre Michael Brown's brother, Harry, stood conversing with an officer. "You don't understand! Michael couldn't have made it back in the device without the Excalibur code! He's lost in time!" The officer said something in reply that Lizzie didn't quite catch. "Of course, he didn't steal it! He's a technician not a bloody agent! He's a good person not an enemy of the state!" With that the officer shook her head, moving away from him. Harry Brown gritted his teeth and looked to the television that had been moved into the room, where the journalists were following up on the only story worth reporting, the capture of Elijah Ainsley.

Lizzie marched up to him. "Harry Brown?" She demanded. He recognised her immediately and the bafflement that appeared on his face almost made her laugh. At least his brother had had the good manners to not just stare at her. She slapped a letter into his hand. Elizabeth had received a similar one a few days ago from Elijah, and he had asked her to take this one to his brother, a goodbye of sorts.

Harry looked to the letter with confusion, opening it carefully, he read every word with rapturous attention, tears began to spring in his eyes as he neared the end. As he finally finished, he stared at her before flicking his gaze back to the to where Elijah Ainsley was being led out of his house in handcuffs. A brilliant smile covered the inventors face, as the world watched on at the man who had been their unknown god for forty years. "Michael?" Harry whispered quietly as he watched the stranger.

Lizzie looked from away from the man breaking down in front of her, and back to the broken C.A.L.I.G.O device. The authorities could look all they liked for the small prism that housed the most powerful piece of code ever written but they wouldn't find it. The Excalibur code was not missing, or in enemy hands, it was still atop C.A.L.I.G.O, just forty years in the past, but now no one could go back and change it. History's open door closed finally.

Printed in Great Britain
by Amazon